BOOK REVIEWS

Here's what people are saying:

Fun, from its cover picture featuring Jeremy and a bag of Big Bubba gum to its on-target conclusion.

from BOOKLIST

Breezy dialogue, a fast pace, and lots of humor will make this book pop.

from KIRKUS REVIEWS

GERMY BLEW IT

by Rebecca C. Jones

E. P. DUTTON   NEW YORK

Published by arrangement with
E.P. Dutton, a subsidiary of NAL Penguin Inc.
Weekly Reader is a trademark of Field Publications.

Library of Congress Cataloging in Publication Data

Jones, Rebecca C.
  Germy blew it

  Summary: Dying to get on television and become
famous, Jeremy Bluett tries all sorts of schemes.
  [1. Fame—Fiction.   2. Contests—Fiction]   I. Title.
PZ7.J72478Ge   1987   [Fic]   86–19950
ISBN 0-525-44294-4

Published in the United States by E. P. Dutton,
2 Park Avenue, New York, N.Y. 10016,
a subsidiary of NAL Penguin Inc.

Published simultaneously in Canada by
Fitzhenry & Whiteside Limited, Toronto

Editor: Julie Amper   Designer: Jean Krulis

Printed in the U.S.A.   W   First Edition
10 9 8 7 6 5 4 3 2

for my sister Diana,
whose strength I admire
and whose friendship I cherish

1.

Jeremy picked at the creamed chicken on his plate.

"May I be excused?" he asked. "I don't feel so good."

Mrs. Bluett looked at her son carefully. "What's wrong, Jeremy?"

"I don't know. I just don't feel good."

Dad looked at Jeremy. "He looks all right to me."

Jeremy sucked in his breath and hoped that would make him look pale and pasty.

"I hope he's not coming down with something," Mom said.

"It's the creamed chicken," said Robin, who was eight and a real pain in the butt. "He hates creamed chicken."

"That's not true," Jeremy said. "Creamed chicken is one of my favorite meals."

Robin snorted.

Jeremy ignored her. "May I be excused?" he asked again, very weakly.

"Of course," Mom said. "Go upstairs and lie down."

Jeremy went upstairs to the bathroom and opened the medicine chest. He removed the thermometer from its black case and wrapped it in tissue. Then he took it to

1

his room and placed it carefully in his pencil case, where it would be safe.

He tiptoed to the telephone in his parents' bedroom and dialed Squirrel Hutchison's number.

"Hello," he whispered.

"Germy?" Squirrel asked. "Is that you?"

Only new kids called Jeremy Bluett by his real name. Everybody else called him Germy Blew It.

"How's it going?" Jeremy asked.

"I haven't done anything yet," Squirrel said. "I thought I'd wait until morning to get sick."

"I laid a little groundwork tonight," Jeremy said. "I said I didn't feel good, and I didn't finish dinner."

"Good idea," Squirrel said. "Too bad I can't do it."

"Why can't you?"

"We're having spaghetti."

"So?"

"I *like* spaghetti."

Jeremy sighed.

"But don't worry," Squirrel added quickly. "I'll be sick in the morning."

"You'd better. You wouldn't want to be the only one at school tomorrow."

After he hung up, Jeremy tiptoed back to his room, changed into his pajamas and started putting together a night bag—equipped with a flashlight, five Masters of the Universe comics, nine pieces of Big Bubba bubble gum, and a bag of Cheetos. He'd saved the Cheetos for an emergency like this.

Jeremy was in bed with the lights off when Robin came up the stairs. He lay there quietly, sucking on Cheetos. Munching would have made too much noise.

There were only two Cheetos left by the time Jeremy heard his parents on the stairs. He closed his eyes and started breathing very slowly, in and out, in and out.

Mom opened his door and walked over to Jeremy's bed.

Jeremy kept breathing, in and out, in and out.

She touched his forehead.

In and out, in and out.

"How is he?" Dad asked from the door.

In and out, in and out.

"I can't tell," Mom said. "You know, I could always tell when they were little. But they're growing so fast." She sighed and walked back toward the door. "What'll we do if he can't go to school tomorrow?"

"Don't worry," Dad said. "He'll be fine."

They closed the door, but Jeremy stayed quiet until the toilet had flushed twice and the hall light had gone out.

Then he popped a piece of Big Bubba in his mouth and pulled out his flashlight and comics.

Mom was standing over Jeremy's bed when he woke up. "How do you feel?" she asked.

Jeremy moaned and buried his head under the covers.

She turned and left the room. From under the covers, he could hear her heels *click-click*ing down the hall and into the bathroom. He heard the medicine chest open.

"Does anybody know where the thermometer is?" she called.

Nobody answered.

"Why do these things always happen when I'm in a hurry?" Nobody answered that, either, and she *click-*

*click*ed back to Jeremy's room. She put her hand under the covers and felt his forehead. "I can't tell," she said. "Do you hurt anywhere?"

Jeremy nodded weakly.

"Where?"

"Everywhere." Jeremy spoke softly so his voice would sound sick. Then he coughed. A weak, sickly cough.

She saw a Big Bubba wrapper on his sheet.

"What's this doing here?" she asked. She looked around, checking for gum on the carpet.

"My stomach hurt," Jeremy said, hoping she wouldn't look under the bed and see the empty bag of Cheetos. "I thought I might throw up, but the gum made me feel better."

She sighed. "Think of your teeth, Jeremy."

He ran his tongue over his teeth. They felt fine.

"Hank!" Mom called. "Come see what you think."

Dad came to the door. "Get out of bed, Jeremy. Let's have a look at you."

Jeremy rolled, weakly, out of bed.

"Does he have a fever?" Dad asked.

"I don't know. I can't find the thermometer."

"What do *you* think, Jeremy?" Dad asked. "Do you think you should go to school?" Mr. Bluett always liked to involve his children in the decision-making process. That way, he said, they would grow up to be Quick Thinkers.

But Jeremy didn't want to look like a Quick Thinker now. He wanted to look sick. So he shrugged, weakly.

"I don't know, Sal," Dad said. "It's up to you."

"This is awful," Mom said. "Bill is counting on me to come in early today, and Mrs. Carlson won't take him if he's sick." She looked at her husband.

4

"Don't look at me like that," he said. "I told you I'm meeting a new client today."

Jeremy summoned the strength to make a suggestion. "I could stay by myself."

"I've never left you alone for a whole day," Mom said, "and I'm not going to start when you're sick."

"Other kids do it. All the time."

"He *is* in the fifth grade," Dad said.

Mom hesitated, and Jeremy held his breath.

"Would you rather send him to school when he's sick?" Dad asked.

Mom looked at her watch, then at Jeremy. "Maybe if I call you during the day . . ."

It worked. The Fifth Grade Strike was on.

2.

Jeremy tried to imagine Mrs. Scheeler's face when she walked into the classroom and saw all those empty seats. She'd probably run to the principal's office.

"Ms. Morrison, come quickly!" Mrs. Scheeler cries.

"Why? What's wrong?" Ms. Morrison asks.

"My class is gone! Vanished!"

Together they run back to Room 5-B.

"Where could they be?" Ms. Morrison asks.

"Look!" Mrs. Scheeler says. "There's a note taped to the side of the supply cabinet." She rips off the note and begins reading: " '5-B is on strike until Dolley Madison Elementary School starts scheduling field trips again. Lack of money is no excuse. How do you expect kids to learn anything when they're bored stiff?' " She examines the note carefully. "Jeremy Bluett wrote this. I'd recognize his penmanship anywhere."

"Is this the same Jeremy Bluett who circulated the petition last fall about the cafeteria food?" Ms. Morrison asks.

Mrs. Scheeler nods and smiles, just thinking of him. "He's a wonderful boy."

6

"Well," Ms. Morrison says, "the pizza is awfully dry. I've been meaning to speak to the cook." She hangs her head in shame, then brightens. "Let's call Jeremy right away and thank him for pointing out the necessity of field trips. I had no idea they were so important to the educational process."

Mrs. Scheeler nods again. "If money is a problem, I can take a pay cut."

"And I can, too," Ms. Morrison says. "Now, let's call Jeremy and give him the good news."

Jeremy didn't think pay cuts would be necessary. He didn't mind cheap field trips. In fact, his all-time favorite class trip had been to Quincy's Meat Locker, where he'd seen huge sides of beef hanging from the ceiling and dripping real blood onto the floor.

Just thinking of the meat locker made Jeremy hungry. He might as well eat breakfast while he waited for Ms. Morrison's call. He went downstairs and found a bowl of Cheerios waiting for him on the kitchen table. An ordinary breakfast for an ordinary day.

But this was a special day, and it called for a special breakfast.

He looked in the refrigerator. Maybe he'd make pancakes, blueberry pancakes.

But he didn't know how to make blueberry pancakes.

There must be a recipe somewhere. His mother always said if you could read, you could cook.

Jeremy eyed the cookbooks, up on a high shelf. What a stupid place to keep cookbooks. Even his mother couldn't reach them without climbing on a chair.

He pulled over a chair, climbed up, and began reading the titles: *Leone's Italian Cookbook, A Cookbook for Lovers* (good grief, Jeremy thought), *Mastering the Art of French*

Cooking. None of these sounded like pancakes. Then he saw *Joy of Cooking.* That might have it.

As he pulled down the book, he spotted a shiny brown bag tucked behind *A Cookbook for Lovers.* It looked like—yes, it was—a bag of M & M's.

Jeremy couldn't believe it. His mother—the one who pushed vitamin pills, lectured about the evils of chewing Big Bubba, and refused to buy Twinkies for their lunches —his mother kept M & M's stashed behind her cookbooks.

He thought of all the times she'd pursed her lips and paused before answering a question. He'd always thought she was thinking things over, but, no, she was just sucking on an M & M.

He opened the bag. Forget the pancakes. He'd have M & M's for breakfast.

Ms. Morrison hadn't called by the time Jeremy finished the M & M's. Maybe they hadn't found the note yet.

He chewed Big Bubba and played Missile Command on the Atari while he waited. He blasted lasers all over the TV screen and scored a new career high of 67,395 points.

The telephone still didn't ring. He thought about calling Squirrel and some of the other strikers, but he didn't want Ms. Morrison to get a busy signal when she called him.

He popped another piece of Big Bubba in his mouth. He wished he'd put something in the note about letting students chew gum in class. Whenever Mrs. Scheeler found somebody chewing gum, she made him stick it on his nose.

The telephone still didn't ring. Maybe Mrs. Scheeler

didn't recognize his handwriting. Jeremy should have signed his name.

Finally, at eleven thirty, the telephone rang. Jeremy took the Big Bubba out of his mouth before he answered it.

"Hello."

"Hi, honey." It wasn't Ms. Morrison. It was Mom. The M & M junkie.

"How are you feeling?" she asked.

Jeremy groaned. He didn't know how long this strike would have to last.

"I'll try to come home early," she said. "By the way, I don't suppose you've found the thermometer."

"Uh, no."

"I'd better buy a new one on the way home."

Jeremy wondered how much thermometers cost. They looked pretty fragile, so they must be expensive.

"Don't do that," he said. "Let me look for it first." He was pretty sure he'd find it.

3.

The telephone rang again around three o'clock. It was Squirrel. "You're not really sick, are you?" he asked.

"Of course not."

"I just wondered. You were the only one absent today."

"The only one! But the whole class was supposed to be on strike!"

"Even Margaret Jagodinski came back from her pink-eye."

"You're kidding!"

"No, the doctor said it wasn't contagious anymore."

Jeremy sighed. Sometimes Squirrel was a little slow. "*Nobody* stayed home?"

"No, but don't worry. I took your note off the supply cabinet before Mrs. Scheeler had a chance to see it. And I got your makeup work for you. But then I remembered that you didn't take your books home."

"No," Jeremy said stiffly. "*I* was on strike."

"That's what I called about," Squirrel said. "The strike."

"Why? What happened?"

"Make sure you watch the Channel 2 news at six. You won't believe it."

"Believe what?" Jeremy asked.

"Just watch."

So Jeremy watched. He told his mother it was a class assignment and he had to watch. Mrs. Bluett always got excited when she thought Jeremy was doing homework. She brought a TV tray into the family room so he could eat dinner and watch at the same time.

"How come he gets to eat in here?" asked Robin. "He's not *that* sick."

"The teacher wants him to watch the news tonight," Mom said. "They're probably studying current events."

Robin still looked suspicious. "I bet he'll change channels while we're gone."

But Jeremy wouldn't do that. Not when Squirrel told him to watch.

"By the way, Jeremy," Mom said, "you didn't use one of my cookbooks today, did you?"

Jeremy swallowed. "Me? I've been sick all day."

"I know. It's just that I seem to have misplaced something."

"What?" As if he didn't know.

"Uh, just some medicine. Don't worry about it, though. I've got more."

Good grief, Jeremy thought. She must have M & M's stashed all over the house.

As soon as she left the room, he lifted a sofa cushion. But he didn't find any M & M's.

Channel 2's news began with a story about the mayor, then one about some truck drivers going on strike. Then there was a First National Bank commercial. When the

news came back on, there was something about the
school board budget.

Then Squirrel's face came on the tube. His old buddy
Squirrel. And he was talking into a microphone that said
CHANNEL 2's FOR YOU on it.

"How do you feel about your school cancelling all field
trips?" a voice asked.

Squirrel grinned at the camera. "I think it's the pits."

"Why?" the voice asked.

Squirrel kept right on grinning at the camera. "Field trips
are fun."

"Squirrel!" Jeremy yelled.

Mom came running. "What's wrong? Are you all
right?"

"Squirrel!" He pointed to the screen.

She looked and smiled. "Why, it's Karen Clark."

Jeremy looked back at the screen. She was right. Squirrel was gone, and Karen Clark was there, giggling like
always, only this time into a microphone.

"Hank! Robin!" Mom called. "Come quickly! Some of
Jeremy's friends are on TV!"

Jeremy was so excited that he didn't even mind her
calling Karen Clark his friend. Dad and Robin came running, and they all watched Karen giggle some more.

"What's this all about?" Mom asked.

"It probably has something to do with the school budget cuts," Dad said. Mr. Bluett always knew what was
going on because he worked in the advertising depart-
ment of *The Advocate-Journal.*

The picture on the screen changed again; it showed
Jeremy's whole class, looking very busy, like maybe

they were taking a test. There was just one empty desk.

"It's too bad you were sick today," Mom said.

"Your one chance to be on TV, and you blew it." Robin smiled sweetly.

"Well, those are the breaks," Dad said as he headed back to his dinner.

Jeremy pounded his fist into a pillow. It wasn't fair! He should have been the one to tell that microphone how important field trips are. He was the one—the only one —who'd cared enough to go on strike!

The telephone rang. Jeremy knew it would be Squirrel.

"Did you see me? Did you? What'd you think?"

"Yeah," Jeremy said. "It was great."

"I wonder how many people saw me. My dad says it's the top-rated station in town. And it goes out on cable."

"Yeah, but a lot of people probably missed it," Jeremy said. "I mean, it came on when they were eating dinner."

"Everybody I know watched it," Squirrel said. "Either they were at school today and knew about it, or I called them. My mom even called my grandmother in Florida, and she doesn't even get Channel 2. But how many times does a guy get a chance to be on TV?"

Jeremy wondered.

"Why'd they come to our class?" he asked.

"Kevin Johansen told his aunt about the field trip strike. She works at Channel 2 and told some reporters about it. They said they're always looking for unusual stories."

"But there wasn't a strike."

"I know." Squirrel laughed. "That's the funny part."

Jeremy didn't think it was funny.

"You don't *mind* my being on TV, do you, Germy?

They asked who organized the protest, but you weren't there."

"No, I don't mind," Jeremy lied. "You did a good job."

Then he hung up the telephone and pounded the pillow again.

4.

When Jeremy walked into 5-B the next morning, everybody was talking about their night on the news.

"Did you see me?" Mary Kate Williams said. "My hair was sticking out like this." She pulled her hair straight out from her head. "I could have died."

Jeremy hadn't noticed Mary Kate's hair—or Mary Kate, for that matter. She must have been one of the kids taking the test at the end.

"What kind of test was it?" he asked Squirrel.

"What test?"

"It looked like you were taking a test on TV."

"Oh, that. The cameraman told us to look busy, and we did. It was part of the package."

"Package?"

"You know," Squirrel said, "the story they put together in the editing booth."

Jeremy didn't know what an editing booth was. Was it like a phone booth, and did the TV people roll it into the classroom? He wanted to ask Squirrel, but Squirrel was too busy telling everyone about all the phone calls his family got last night from people who'd seen him on TV. Even his old nursery school teacher had called.

Jeremy decided to wait until lunch to ask about the editing booth. Normally he and Squirrel did their best talking in the cafeteria line. It kept them from thinking too much about what might be on the trays ahead.

But Squirrel was busy in the cafeteria line, too, telling everyone why he and Karen Clark had been chosen to speak for the class.

"It's simple," Squirrel said. "They wanted kids who could talk good."

"Oh, sure, Squirrel, you're a great talker!" David Jones said. Some other kids laughed, too. But they saved a seat for Squirrel in the cafeteria.

Nobody saved a seat for Jeremy. Not that he expected them to. *He* hadn't been on TV.

Jeremy looked down at the pizza on his tray. It looked dry and pink. He wondered where the school managed to find pink pizza. Even the frozen pizzas from the store turn out red and gooey when you cook them.

A couple of fourth grade girls looked at him and giggled behind their hands. Jeremy knew what they were saying.

"There's old Germy Blew It. Did you hear how he missed being on TV?"

"Oh, is he the one who thought up the strike?"

"Yeah, but nobody stayed home. Everybody came to school and got on TV."

"Everybody but old Germy Blew It."

They both nod sympathetically.

"I kinda feel sorry for Germy."

"Me, too."

Jeremy sat down and, with great dignity, began chewing on his dry, pink pizza.

"Where were you at lunch?" Squirrel asked on the way home. "I didn't see you."

"Oh, I was around," Jeremy said.

"Well, you should have seen what Kevin Johansen had for lunch. Twinkies, Hostess Cup Cakes, and Ho-Hos."

"You're kidding."

"And a carton of Hawaiian Punch."

"No sandwich or carrot or anything like that?" Jeremy was impressed. His mother—the M & M junkie—didn't pack lunches often, but when she did, they were always stuffed with vitamins.

"He says that's what he's going to be bringing from now on," Squirrel said. "His dad just got a job driving a Hostess delivery truck, and he's going to give Kevin all the stuff that's smushed."

"Oh." Still, a smushed Twinkie was better than dry pizza. The only thing Mr. Bluett ever brought home from work was a free newspaper.

"Kevin said he'd bring something extra for me tomorrow." Squirrel looked at Jeremy, then added quickly, "Don't worry, though. I'll save some for you."

That did it. Even Squirrel was feeling sorry for him.

Jeremy had to get himself on TV.

5.

After school, Robin and Jeremy always went to Mrs. Carlson's house, which was around the corner and three houses down from the Bluetts. Two third grade girls also went there after school, and two little kids stayed there all day. Mrs. Carlson always said Jeremy was the only boy at her house who could be counted on to keep his pants dry.

Jeremy wished she wouldn't say that.

Mrs. Carlson had a lot of rules. Jeremy was not allowed to play with Squirrel, even though Squirrel lived right next door to her. And he wasn't allowed to chew Big Bubba or watch TV, either. Mrs. Carlson said there hadn't been a decent show on television since Lawrence Welk went off the air.

Mrs. Carlson played Lawrence Welk's records every day. She said he was the greatest musician of our times. But Jeremy liked Michael Jackson better.

Mrs. Bluett said maybe next year Jeremy and Robin could go to their own house after school and take care of themselves. Maybe.

Jeremy wished it were next year already. Especially

today. He had an important phone call to make. And another one of Mrs. Carlson's rules was that he couldn't use the telephone.

It was four thirty when Mrs. Bluett picked up Jeremy and Robin. And it was five o'clock by the time she and Robin went upstairs to change clothes, leaving Jeremy alone in the kitchen with the telephone.

He looked for Channel 2's phone number in the telephone directory. He didn't find it. So he dialed information.

"What's Channel 2's phone number?" he asked the operator.

"I have no listing for Channel 2," she said. "Are you sure that's the correct name?"

"Of course I'm sure. Don't you watch TV?" What a stupid operator. Jeremy hung up.

But then he started thinking. Maybe Channel 2 *did* have another name. *W* something.

He went into the family room and turned on the TV, softly so Mom and Robin wouldn't hear it. He wasn't supposed to watch TV at home, either, until his homework was finished. He sat through ten minutes of "Flippo the Clown" before there was a station break.

"Channel 2's for you," the announcer said. "WQQP-TV."

Jeremy ran back to the telephone and dialed information again. A different operator came on the line.

"Do you have a listing for WQQP-TV?"

"555–2222."

Jeremy had to dial the number three times because he kept losing track of the number of *2*'s, but he finally got it right and a woman's voice answered.

"Channel 2's for you," she said.

"Hello." Jeremy tried to speak from the bottom of his throat so his voice would sound deeper. "My name is Jeremy Bluett, and I have some more information on the story you did yesterday on—"

"Just a moment, please." She cut him off, and a tape recording came on, with people singing:

> Channel 2's the one for you!
> Channel 2's the one for me!
> Channel 2's the one for everyone
> Who wa-a-atches TV!
> Channel 2's the one for you!
> Channel 2's the one for—

A man interrupted the singing. "Newsroom, Peterson."

"Hello. My name is Jeremy Bluett, and I have some more information about the story you did at Dolley Madison Elementary School yesterday. See, I wasn't—"

"Just a minute." Peterson evidently held his hand over the phone while he talked to someone else. Then he came back on the line. "He's not here now. Do you want to leave your number?"

Jeremy didn't know who wasn't there, but he gave Peterson his phone number anyway.

Mrs. Bluett and Robin were still upstairs when the telephone rang, and Jeremy answered it.

"This is Tom Boyd from Channel 2 news," a voice said. "I have a message to call Jeremy Blute."

"Bluett," Jeremy corrected him. "That's me, and I called because I have more information about that

20

story you did yesterday at Dolley Madison Elementary School."

"Yeah?"

"Yeah." Jeremy lowered his voice again. "See, you came to my classroom yesterday when I wasn't there. I was on strike."

"When I was a kid, we called it playing hooky."

"Oh, no," Jeremy said. "The whole class was supposed to be on strike, but I was the only one who pulled it off."

"Does your teacher know that's why you stayed home?"

"Not exactly, but . . ."

"Do your parents know? Does the principal?"

"Uh, no."

"That's hooky, kid."

"I guess that means you don't want to . . . uh . . . interview me," Jeremy said.

Tom Boyd didn't say anything. He just laughed and hung up.

At dinner Jeremy asked his father how reporters pick their stories.

Mr. Bluett leaned back in his chair. He always liked to talk about the reporters at *The Advocate-Journal.* He had majored in journalism in college and wanted to be a reporter. But then he found out that reporters get paid peanuts.

When Jeremy was little, he thought it would be great to go to work and get some peanuts. Then he got older and figured out what his father meant.

"Reporters work hard," Dad said. "They have to check

21

with a lot of people every day. The police, the mayor, the school board. Lots of people. And they have tó keep their eyes and ears open all the time. Sometimes they hear about stories from contacts they've developed, and sometimes—"

"Contacts?"

"People they've talked to on other stories."

"Like Squirrel?"

"Squirrel?" Dad looked puzzled.

"Sure, Squirrel was on Channel 2 news last night. Remember?"

Dad chuckled. "I guess Channel 2 would consider Squirrel a contact. If anything big ever happens at Dolley Madison Elementary School, they'll call Squirrel right away."

Robin became interested. "Do you mean Squirrel could get us all on TV?"

"Well, he'd have to have a story. And it would have to be a good one, not something they'd already done."

"Yeah," Jeremy said. "If you call up a TV station and tell them about a story they've already done, they'll laugh at you."

"Why would Squirrel call a TV station and tell them about a story they've already done?" Robin asked. "Squirrel's not *that* stupid."

6.

Jeremy looked out his window Tuesday morning and saw a fresh layer of snow. He turned on the radio and listened for school cancellations, but there weren't any. He wasn't surprised. He figured out a long time ago that their school superintendent must have been raised in an Eskimo village. Snow never bothered him. He'd send kids out in sixteen feet of the stuff.

Mrs. Carlson called.

"Oh, I'm sorry to hear that," Mrs. Bluett said. "You probably have what Jeremy had. It only lasts a day, but you need to take care of yourself. I hope you feel better soon."

Mrs. Bluett hung up the phone and frowned. Jeremy knew it was time for Other Arrangements.

Jeremy liked Other Arrangements. Other Arrangements meant one of his parents would try to leave work early and come home. In the meantime, he and Robin could go to their own house after school and stay by themselves. They had to keep the doors locked and tell anyone who called that their mother was in the shower and couldn't come to the phone right now.

Otherwise they could do what they wanted. They could watch TV or play Missile Command or call people on the telephone. Sometimes Jeremy called a weather recording, sometimes he called Dial-a-Prayer, and sometimes he just leafed through the phone book and called the first name his finger landed on. If somebody answered, he asked if her refrigerator was running.

Most people hung up right away, but sometimes somebody would say yes.

"Then you'd better go catch it," Jeremy would say, and hang up quickly.

Other Arrangements were fun. They were almost as good as having school cancelled because of snow.

Mrs. Bluett always dropped off Jeremy and Robin on her way to work in the morning. When it snowed, though, she dropped them off two blocks from the school.

"Your boots can climb that hill better than this car can," she said.

Jeremy didn't mind. He liked making tracks in the snow.

A cold wind rushed at him as he got out of the car. Jeremy didn't mind that, either. It made him feel like he was on an important Arctic mission.

Robin minded, though. "Ooo-oooh," she cried, and she didn't move.

Jeremy walked on ahead, toward the North Pole.

"Jeremeeee!" Robin wailed. "Don't leave me here!"

Arctic explorers don't leave little kids behind. Especially when their mother is watching and worrying about Other Arrangements. Jeremy turned back and took Robin's hand. He pulled her through the wind.

If only a TV camera were around.

"Ten-year-old Jeremy Bluett rescued his little sister, Robin, in a freezing windstorm this morning. Robin later told reporters that Jeremy's quick thinking and heroic efforts saved her life. We'll have an interview with Jeremy at eleven."

But there weren't any TV cameras around, and Robin didn't even thank him for saving her life.

Jeremy jammed his fists deep into his pockets—and felt an interesting lump in the lining of his jacket. He kept poking until he found a hole in his pocket that his finger could wiggle through. He used the hole to explore the unknown territory between his jacket and its lining. He pulled out a lot of lint before he found the lump.

It was a piece of Big Bubba, stiff and cold. Probably left over from last winter.

All morning Jeremy rolled the old Big Bubba between his fingers and tried to think of heroic things he could do to get himself on TV. Maybe he could catch a bank robber or a kidnapper. Maybe he could save a little kid from drowning. Or maybe he could set some sort of world record.

But where would he find a bank robber or a kidnapper or a drowning kid? And what would he do with them if he found them? Jeremy didn't even know how to swim. And there was nothing he could do faster or better than anyone else. What kind of world record could he set?

Jeremy wished he could talk to Squirrel about this. Sometimes just talking to Squirrel gave him ideas. But Squirrel had been eating lunch lately with Kevin Johansen and his Twinkies. And Jeremy had avoided them because he knew Squirel would offer to share a Twinkie out of pity.

The Big Bubba was getting soft between his fingers. He propped up his social studies book as a shield and unwrapped it. Then, pretending to yawn, he covered his mouth with his hand and slipped the Big Bubba onto his tongue.

"Jeremy."

Jeremy's heart took the extra beat it always took when a teacher called his name.

"You weren't listening, were you, Jeremy?" Mrs. Scheeler said.

Jeremy didn't say anything. He knew he couldn't speak without Mrs. Scheeler guessing there was something in his mouth.

"Okay, Jeremy, one more time: What freedoms are guaranteed by the First Amendment?"

The First Amendment sounded familiar.

Mrs. Scheeler sighed. "All right, Karen." She nodded to a raised hand. "What are they?"

"Freedom of worship, freedom of the press, freedom of assembly, freedom of petition, and freedom of speech," Karen said.

"That's right, Karen. Sometimes we lump all those freedoms together and call them freedom of expression." Mrs. Scheeler turned back to Jeremy. "Try to stay with us, okay, Jeremy?"

Jeremy tried. He looked down at his book, which was open to a picture of George Washington with his head in the clouds. Good old George Washington. *He* never had trouble thinking of something heroic to do.

"George Washington and Jeremy Bluett started a revolution at Dolley Madison Elementary School this morning. Jeremy presented a list of grievances to school principal Judith Morrison, and General Washington threatened military action if Ms. Morrison did not meet Jeremy's demands. Those demands would guarantee students four field trips a month, the right to chew gum in class, a guaranteed number of snow days each winter, and a choice of foods in the cafeteria. We'll have live interviews with both General Washington and Jeremy at eleven."

"Jeremy."

Jeremy's heart took that extra beat again.

Mrs. Scheeler sighed. "I thought you were going to stay with us, Jeremy."

"I was," Jeremy said. "I mean, I am."

Too late, he remembered that he shouldn't speak.

"Oh, Jeremy, not again," Mrs. Scheeler said. "Well, you know what to do with it."

Everyone turned to watch as Jeremy took the Big Bubba out of his mouth and stuck it on his nose. He felt his cheeks grow hot.

"Now, what's the answer to the question, Jeremy?"

Jeremy looked past the gum on his nose to the picture of George Washington, but that was no help. George's head was still in the clouds.

"All right, Mary Kate, what do we call our elected officials in Congress?"

Mary Kate smiled at Jeremy. "Senators and representatives."

Jeremy smiled back. He had an idea.

7.

It was a good thing there were Other Arrangements today. Jeremy didn't have time to waste listening to old Lawrence Welk records. He had to dash home from school, find the key under the old geranium pot, unlock the door, and call Channel 2.

Peterson said Tom Boyd wasn't there again, but he'd leave a message for him.

Jeremy sat down to wait.

Robin wanted to go outside and build a snowman.

"We're supposed to stay inside," Jeremy said.

"Mom said it would be okay if we went out together and stayed in our yard," Robin said.

"When did she say that?"

"When I called her. Just a minute ago."

"Don't use the phone!" Jeremy said. "I'm waiting for an important call."

Robin smiled. "I won't make any calls if I'm outside building a snowman," she said. "But if I have to stay inside . . ."

"All right, all right." Jeremy put on his coat and mittens and went outside with Robin. He stayed on the front

28

step while she made a pathetic little snowman, about eighteen inches high.

"Jeremeee!" she kept calling. "I need your help!"

But Jeremy wouldn't leave the front step. He had to be able to hear the phone when it rang.

It didn't ring.

When his mother's car pulled into the driveway at 3:55, Jeremy didn't stick around to tell his version of how the Other Arrangements had worked. He ran inside and called the station again. This time Tom Boyd was there.

"I called earlier, but I guess you didn't get my message," Jeremy said.

"I got it, all right," Tom Boyd said, "but I recognized your name."

"I think I've got a story for you," Jeremy said. "Something new this time."

"What is it?" Tom Boyd's voice sounded tired.

"I'm, uh, starting this new campaign."

"Yeah, what is it?"

"I, uh, want kids to be able to, um, vote."

"Kids? Vote? You mean, like for president? They've already lowered the voting age to eighteen, and I don't think they'll go any lower."

"No," Jeremy said, "not that kind of voting. I want kids to be able to vote on stuff at school."

"What kind of stuff?"

"Like homework and cafeteria food and stuff like that."

"Do you mean you think there ought to be a student representative on the school board?"

That sounded good. "Yeah," Jeremy said.

"Well, there already *is* a student on the board. They've

29

had one for fifteen years. If you've got some complaints, you should take them to her. And do me a favor, Jeremy."

"Yeah?"

"Stop calling me."

On the front page, *The Advocate-Journal* had a big picture of a couple of kids building a snowman. Robin looked at it wistfully. "I could have made one like that," she said, "if Jeremy had helped."

She was right. If Jeremy had worked on a snowman—instead of listening for the stupid phone to ring—they could have made the biggest and best snowman in town.

Maybe Channel 2 would have come out and interviewed them while they made it.

He looked through the rest of the newspaper to see what other stories he'd missed. There was a lot of stuff about deficits. It seemed like everybody—the president, the governor, even some shoppers at the mall—had something to say about deficits. Jeremy wasn't sure what deficits were.

And there was a story about a kid in Cleveland who had her own TV talk show. Her own TV show! How lucky can a kid get? And it wasn't even her first time on TV. The story said this kid had been on before—when she went to visit the governor. It seems the governor invited her to the statehouse because he liked a letter she wrote.

Jeremy put down the newspaper. His own TV show. And all he had to do was write a letter.

He went upstairs to his room and took out the box of lined stationery Aunt Loretta had given him for Christmas. In the bottom right corner of each sheet was a cartoon of a fish saying "Drop me a line sometime." It seemed a little silly for writing such an important letter, but it was all he had.

Now, who should he write? That kid in Cleveland had already taken the governor, so he'd have to try somebody else. Maybe he could write the lieutenant governor, or the governor of another state. No, that would just look like he was copying.

And, besides, why bother with a governor? He should go straight to the top and write the president of the United States. But what should he write about? Jeremy chewed on his pencil eraser for a while, then began.

> Dear Mr. President,
>   I am very concerned about the country, and I would like to have a talk with you. Please let me know when it would be convenient for me to visit.
>
> > Sincerely,
> > Jeremy Bluett

Jeremy looked at the letter. It needed more punch. So he wrote:

> P.S. I'd especially like to talk with you about the deficits. I have some good ideas about what to do with them.

There. That was better. He folded the paper and put it in an envelope.

But the president probably got a lot of letters, Jeremy thought. It wouldn't hurt to write another world leader. Like maybe the head of China or Germany. But Jeremy didn't know the names of those leaders, or where they lived. And he didn't know any foreign words, except maybe *chop suey* or *Volkswagen*. He'd better write somebody in English.

Jeremy could think of only one other world leader who knew English. So he wrote her.

Dear Queen Elizabeth,
    I am a ten-year-old American, but I am very interested in England. (I am also very interested in deficits.) I would like to come visit you, if you have time.

Sincerely,
Jeremy Bluett

8.

Jeremy asked his father at dinner if he'd ever been on TV.

"Once," he said. "I was at an Ohio State basketball game, and my parents were watching the game on TV. My mother said she saw me in the crowd."

"Did they show you close up?" Jeremy asked.

"I don't think so," Dad said. "My father wasn't sure it was me."

"I was on TV once," Mrs. Bluett said. "I was interviewed."

Jeremy looked at his mother with new respect. "You were *interviewed*? With a microphone and camera and everything?"

She nodded.

Mr. Bluett laughed. "Oh, I remember this story."

"What story? What happened?" Jeremy didn't know his mother had been a celebrity.

"Well, I was four years old."

Robin giggled.

"And my father took me to the St. Patrick's Day parade

in Chicago—the one where they dye the Chicago River green. I wonder if they still do that."

"How do they dye a river green?" Robin asked.

"Who cares?" Jeremy said. "Tell us how you got on TV."

"Well," Mrs. Bluett said, "there was a big crowd, but people let the little kids stand up front, near the curb, so we could see. I was standing next to a little girl who was waving a Confederate flag."

"At a St. Patrick's Day parade?"

"Yes," Mom said. "That flag evidently attracted the attention of a TV reporter who was there to cover the parade. He didn't have a camera or anything, but he came over and asked her why she had that Confederate flag, and she told him, 'The South shall rise again.' " Mrs. Bluett mimicked a Southern drawl.

"Then the reporter turned to me and asked if I was from the South, too. And I said yes, I was from 9406 *South* Mayfield Avenue. He thought that was pretty cute, so he took the two of us over to a booth they'd set up for the parade, and interviewed us on camera."

"So you were on TV?" Jeremy asked.

"Yes." Mom smiled.

"Tell the rest of it, Sal." Dad was chuckling.

"Why, what happened?" Jeremy asked.

"Nothing much. Would you pass the peas please, Robin?"

"Nothing much!" Dad said. "When they got your mother and the other little girl on camera again, the reporter asked them the same questions. This time when the reporter asked your mother if she was from the South, she said 'No.' The reporter tried to get her to say something cute about *South* Mayfield Avenue, but your mother just stood there and sucked her thumb."

Mom giggled. "My father was really embarrassed."

Jeremy didn't blame him. He was just glad the Bluetts didn't live in Chicago now, where someone might remember that his mother had been such a jerk.

Still, the story gave him an idea.

"Do they ever have parades here?" he asked.

"Oh, sure," Dad said. "They have them on the Fourth of July and Veterans Day and Memorial Day and . . . They may even have one next week for Presidents' Day."

"Next week?" Good old Presidents' Day. The school would be closed.

Robin giggled. "Jeremy wants to be on TV," she said. "He wants to wave a Confederate flag and get on TV."

"I do not," Jeremy said. "I just wondered if they ever have parades here." He turned to his father. "You think they'll have one next week?"

"I don't know," Dad said. "I can ask someone in the newsroom."

"Well, *I'm* not going to a parade, even if they have one," Mrs. Bluett said. "The stores always have terrific Presidents' Day sales, and I need a new winter coat." She looked at her husband. "I was hoping you'd come along. You know how much trouble I have making decisions on things like that."

Mr. Bluett knew. "Gee," he said, "I'd been looking forward to taking the kids to the parade."

"I thought you said you didn't know if the city was having one."

"I'll find out tomorrow."

35

A reporter told Mr. Bluett that there would be a parade at ten o'clock, starting at city hall.

"It's not going to be a big parade," Dad warned at dinner that night. "Just a few high school bands, some veterans and some guy dressed up as George Washington. It's too cold and windy for floats."

"Do you think they'll cover it on TV?" Jeremy asked.

"I'm sure they will. Why, would you rather watch it on TV?"

Robin laughed. "Jeremy wants to *be* on TV."

"No, I don't!" Jeremy said. "I just wanted to know if the parade's important enough to be on TV."

"I don't know how *important* it is," Dad said, "but I'm sure it'll be on TV. Reporters get pretty desperate on holidays, with the city and state offices closed."

Desperate reporters. It was sounding better all the time.

9.

Michael Taylor brought a monkey skin to school on Friday. It had long black fur, and there were two holes where the monkey's eyes used to be. Michael said his uncle brought it back from South America.

After Michael showed the monkey skin to the class, he took it back to his desk and arranged the skin so it made a furry seat cover. He sat on it all morning. Then he took it to the cafeteria at lunchtime. Seven different boys saved seats for him, and he chose the one next to Kevin Johansen. Kevin gave him two Twinkies, and Michael let him sit on the monkey skin.

Squirrel sat next to Jeremy.

"Too bad about your Twinkies," Jeremy said. Jeremy felt a little sorry for Squirrel, especially now that he knew he'd be on TV—if not with the queen or the president, then definitely at the parade.

"Aw, that's okay," Squirrel said. "I didn't want them anyway. Kevin's stuff is kind of stale. And, besides," he said, "I'm getting kind of tired of Kevin."

"Nobody forced you to sit with him."

Squirrel looked at him. "I thought maybe you were mad at me."

"Mad? Why would I be mad?"

"About being on TV. *You* should have been the one on TV that night. I mean, it was your idea to go on strike."

"I wasn't there. Somebody had to take my place, and I'm glad it was you," Jeremy said generously.

"You mean it? You're not mad?"

Jeremy shook his head. "And, besides, I expect to be on TV myself, any day now."

"Good," Squirrel said. "You deserve it."

Jeremy's letter to Queen Elizabeth came back to him unopened. LACK OF SUFFICIENT POSTAGE had been stamped on both the back and front of the envelope.

Oh, well. If the queen wasn't going to chip in for postage, Jeremy knew she'd never pay for his trip to England. At least he still had the president—and the parade.

He looked through his closet for something to wear or carry that TV reporters would notice. He wanted them to come up nice and close to interview him. He didn't want to end up like his father, so far away from the camera that only his mother could pick him out of the crowd.

There was nothing interesting hanging in his closet and nothing interesting on its shelves, unless you counted his old violin or the three-cornered hat his grandmother brought back from Williamsburg two years ago. It was just like the one Washington himself wore, so it would be perfect for a Presidents' Day parade—except it was too small, and Jeremy didn't want to think what the kids in his class would say if they saw him on TV in a three-cornered hat.

Besides, the little girl at the St. Patrick's Day parade had been carrying a Confederate flag. Jeremy needed something different. Something unexpected.

"Are you looking for something?" Mrs. Bluett asked from the doorway.

Jeremy jumped. His mother should get tap shoes, so people could hear her coming.

She looked over his shoulder into the closet. "Maybe you're going to practice your violin, for old time's sake?"

"No," he said quickly, hoping she wouldn't go into her routine about the money she'd spent on that violin. "I'm just cleaning up a little." He picked up some old test papers which had been stuffed in a corner of the closet floor, and threw them away.

Mom smiled. "Sometimes I think there's hope for you yet."

She left, and Jeremy turned back to his closet. Down in the corner where the test papers had been, he spotted something white and sparkly. He pulled it out and blew off the dust balls. It was a sequined glove, just like the one Michael Jackson wore. Squirrel had given it to him the Christmas before last.

Nobody would expect a Michael Jackson glove at a Presidents' Day parade.

But nobody would see it, either. He needed something bigger.

Jeremy looked around his room for something bigger. There was a globe. And a big wooden *J* that his grandfather had carved when he was born. And, covering the wall next to his bed, his poster collection. Most of the posters were of baseball players, but there was one of

Bruce Springsteen. And an old one of Michael Jackson.

Jeremy looked at the sequined white glove in his hand. Maybe if he made a frame from some of the wood scraps in the basement. And maybe if he wore the glove . . .

"Ladies and gentlemen, we are reporting live from the Presidents' Day parade. I have here a young man named Jeremy Bluett who's wearing a complete, authentic Michael Jackson costume and carrying a Michael Jackson poster. Jeremy, can you tell me why you are promoting Michael Jackson on a day when we are supposed to honor such men as George Washington and Abraham Lincoln?"

"Certainly." Jeremy smiles at the camera. "I just want to remind everyone that people like Washington and Lincoln fought to guarantee our freedom of expression—and that includes musical expression. If it weren't for Washington and Lincoln, we'd all be listening to Lawrence Welk instead of Michael Jackson."

"Thank you, Jeremy, for reminding us what America is all about."

Jeremy smiled as he removed the thumbtacks from the Michael Jackson poster.

10.

It snowed again Sunday night.

"Gee, I wonder if they'll have the parade today," Dad said at breakfast.

"You wouldn't go, would you?" Mom asked.

"Why not?"

"It's seventeen degrees out there, and that's not counting the wind-chill factor," she said. "Why don't you come to the mall, where it'll be nice and warm?"

"No, thanks," Dad said. "The kids and I are going to the parade. Right, kids?"

"Right!" Jeremy said.

Robin didn't say anything. She just looked into her bowl of Cheerios.

"Right, Robin?" Dad asked again.

She still didn't say anything.

"I think," Mom said, "that at least one of our children may have been blessed with some common sense."

Robin looked at her and grinned.

"And at least one of our children," Dad said, "likes the idea of an adventure. Right, Jeremy?"

"Right!"

41

"Don't forget to wear an extra sweater," Mom said, "and an extra scarf and an extra pair of socks and—"

"Don't worry, Sal," Dad said. "We'll be fine."

At nine fifteen Jeremy waddled down the stairs in his extra pants, extra sweater, and extra socks. He was carrying the Michael Jackson poster.

"What's that?" Dad asked.

"A Michael Jackson poster," Jeremy said. He held his right hand behind his back. He thought his father should get used to the poster before he saw the sequined white glove.

"And what are you going to do with it?" Dad asked.

"Take it to the parade."

"Why?"

Jeremy thought about telling him about freedom of musical expression, but instead he just said, "I want to."

"But the wind will whip it to shreds."

"No, it won't. See, I stapled it to a piece of plywood."

Dad shrugged. "Okay, put it in the trunk." He handed Jeremy the car keys. "Just remember that I'm not buying a new poster when this one gets ruined."

"Okay."

First they headed toward the mall to drop off Mom and Robin.

"Look at all these cars!" Dad said, as they joined a long line of cars snaking toward the mall. "I'm sure glad *we're* not going to the mall. It'll be packed."

"And warm," Mom said.

Jeremy was warm enough. The car heater was going full blast, and he was sweating under all those layers of clothes.

"Maybe you'll be more comfortable," Dad told Mom,

"but you'll be missing out on the great American tradition of honoring George Washington and Abraham Lincoln and—"

"The traditional thing to do on Presidents' Day," Mom said, "is to shop."

"Shopping on Presidents' Day," Dad muttered. "It's a national disgrace."

A cold wind rushed into the car as Mom opened the door to get out. "Standing outside to watch a parade in weather like this," she said, "is stupid."

Traffic heading toward the center of town was light.

"Good," Dad said. "It'll be easy to find a parking space."

When they got out of the car, Jeremy had to remind his father about the Michael Jackson poster in the trunk.

"Are you sure you want that thing?" Dad asked.

"Yeah," Jeremy said. "It represents how much freedom we have in this country."

Dad rolled his eyes and handed Jeremy the key to unlock the trunk. "Okay, but don't wave it around too much. It might get ripped—and we might see someone I know."

As Jeremy reached into the trunk for the poster, Dad spotted the sequined white glove on his right hand. "What's that for?" he asked.

"It's a symbol of Michael Jackson . . . and our freedom of expression."

"Put your mitten on."

"But Dad . . ."

"Forget it," he said. "Your mother will kill me if I bring you home with a frostbitten hand."

"But . . ."

"It's not too late to go to the mall, Jeremy."

Jeremy put on his mitten.

Then he tucked the poster under his arm and followed his father into the cold wind.

Mr. Bluett said he knew just the spot for watching the parade.

"We'll have a good view, and it shouldn't be too crowded," he said.

He was right about the crowds. One policeman stood on the corner. A few bundled figures hurried down the street, but nobody looked like he was going to stand still long enough to watch a parade.

"Will the parade go by here?" Dad asked the policeman.

"If they don't give up before they get here," the policeman answered, stamping his feet to keep warm.

"What do you mean?"

"Some of the bands have cancelled out because of the weather. They say their instruments won't work right when it's this cold."

"What a bunch of wimps," Dad said. "Think where we'd be today if George Washington had let a little cold weather stop him at Valley Forge."

"I know where I'd be," the policeman said. "I'd be home, in front of the fire."

Jeremy pulled his scarf up to cover his nose and mouth. He held the Michael Jackson poster under his arm and tried to hug himself.

The policeman nodded toward the poster. "What's that for?" he asked.

"It's a Michael Jackson poster," Jeremy said.

Dad sighed.

44

"I can see that," the policeman said. "Why'd you bring it here?"

"So I could hold it during the parade."

"Old Valley Forge here wouldn't buy you a flag?" The policeman looked at Dad. "That's pathetic."

Dad put a firm hand on Jeremy's shoulder. "Maybe we should go home," he said.

"And miss the parade?" Jeremy said. "What about the great American tradition of honoring our presidents? What about Valley Forge?"

With one hand still on Jeremy's shoulder, Dad steered him away from the policeman. "All right," he said. "But stomp your feet, and keep moving. And let me know if you want to go home."

Jeremy stomped his feet. He wasn't going to go home. Not until a TV camera showed up.

11.

Jeremy stood with his back to the wind, stomping his feet, but he was growing numb. The worst part was his toes. He could barely feel them anymore.

And even though he kept the Michael Jackson poster close to his body, the wind kept tugging at it. The paper was tearing away from the staples in several spots.

Dad kept asking if he wanted to go home, but Jeremy kept saying no.

Finally they heard the *rat-a-tat* of distant drums.

"Thank God," Mr. Bluett said.

A few people came to the curb to watch as two slow-moving police cars passed, with their lights flashing.

Behind them marched five or six figures—probably men, but Jeremy couldn't tell for sure because they were bundled beyond recognition. One of the men was carrying an American flag, and Jeremy and his father both stood a little taller as it passed.

Then a drum major, wearing a tall fur hat and waving a baton, led several rows of marching musicians, all wearing royal blue uniforms with brass buttons and gold braid at the shoulders. Their instruments were tucked under their arms as they walked ramrod-stiff behind the drum major. Two drummers beat out the rhythm of their march, *rat-a-tat-tat-tat*.

Jeremy figured the TV camera would be there any minute. He held up his Michael Jackson poster, and he heard it rip some more.

A couple of black cars went by.

"There's the mayor," Mr. Bluett said, pointing to a shadowy figure inside one of the cars.

Then George Washington and Abraham Lincoln rode by on two large brown horses. Washington smiled and pointed out the Michael Jackson poster to Lincoln, who was trying to keep his high hat from blowing away. When he saw the poster, Lincoln laughed and waved to Jeremy. Then both presidents dug their heels into their horses. It looked like they were going to pass the mayor's car.

"I bet those guys are freezing their tails off," Dad said.

A fire truck and a couple more slow-moving police cars followed.

"Well, I guess that's it," Dad said. "Everybody else must have cancelled out."

"What about the TV cameras?" Jeremy asked. "I didn't see any TV cameras."

"They're probably along the route somewhere," Dad said. "Or maybe they got smart and didn't come at all."

"Can we look for them?" Jeremy asked.

"You've got to be kidding," Dad said, and he hurried back toward the car.

Jeremy looked at his poster. Michael Jackson had a big rip over his left eye.

"Guess what!" Robin said as she and Mom got in the car.

"What?" Dad asked.

"Mom and I are going to be on TV tonight!"

Jeremy looked at his mother. She was nodding. It was true.

"Look at Jeremy's face, Mom," Robin said. "I told you he'd die."

"You're going to be on TV?" Dad said. "Why?"

"Channel 2 was doing a story about all the people shopping today," Mom said. "I *told* you the traditional thing to do on Presidents' Day is to shop."

That's right. She did. And Jeremy hadn't listened.

"Did they interview you?" Jeremy asked. "With cameras and microphones and everything?"

Mom nodded.

"Why'd they pick you?"

"I don't know," Mom said. "Maybe we just looked like typical shoppers. Robin wasn't waving a Confederate flag, if that's what you mean."

"So you didn't say anything dumb about being from the South." Dad chuckled.

"No," Mom said. "We played it straight."

"Let's hurry home," Robin said. "I want to call Jennifer and tell her right away. Maybe I should call Melinda, too. And Stacy. Oh, heck, I'll just call everyone in my class."

"How was the parade?" Mom asked.

"Cold," Dad said. "Very cold."

12.

Channel 2 opened its news program with a picture of George Washington and Abraham Lincoln smiling and waving from their horses.

"Good evening. Record low temperatures all but cancelled the city's annual Presidents' Day parade today. Only one high school band marched in the cold, and George Washington and Abraham Lincoln waved to empty sidewalks . . . while people flocked instead to the warm comfort of stores holding their Presidents' Day sales."

"There's Mom! There's Mom!" Robin shouted.
Sure enough, there was Mom.

"My husband and son went to the parade today," Mom said, "but there was no way we were going with them."
"Why not?" a voice asked.
The camera moved down to Robin. "We're not stupid," she said. "It's *cold* out there."

The camera switched to another shopper, marvelling at the low prices.

" *'We're not stupid!'* " Robin cried. "Isn't that great?"

"Words to live by," Dad said.

The telephone rang, and Dad answered it.

"Yes, Bill, it sure was," Dad said. "We sure did. . . . Well, Jeremy had his heart set on it. . . ." Dad laughed. "I guess I do."

He hung up, and the phone rang again. "Yes, Frank, it sure was," he said. "We sure did. . . . Well, Jeremy had his heart set on it." He laughed, not quite as heartily. "I guess I do."

He hung up and turned to his family. "People want to know if I feel *stupid.*" He looked at Robin. "Thanks a lot, kid."

The phone rang again, and Dad answered it with a groan. He smiled, though, when he heard who it was. "It's your turn," he said, handing the receiver to Jeremy.

It was Squirrel. "Was that your mom and Robin on the news?" he asked.

"Yeah."

"They made the top story." Jeremy could tell Squirrel was impressed. "Did you and your dad really go to the parade? In this weather?"

"Uh huh."

"Didn't you freeze?"

"Uh huh."

"You must feel awful," Squirrel said.

"I was okay. I had extra clothes on."

"No, I mean about missing the TV cameras again. I didn't think a guy could miss being on TV twice in a row like that."

Neither did Jeremy.

The phone kept ringing, but Jeremy didn't listen anymore. He went back to the television. There was a story about a cherry pie–eating contest.

"For the fourth year in a row, Chins Dankin won the George Washington Cherry Pie–Eating Contest sponsored by the Tri-State Restaurant Association. Chins ate nine pies in ten minutes, without using a fork or a spoon."

The screen showed Chins, with red syrup smeared across his face and encrusted in his hair, opening his mouth wide and stuffing the last pie down his throat.

Even a slob like Chins Dankin could get on TV—four years in a row.

Jeremy went to bed early again, and this time he really did feel sick. First Squirrel and Karen Clark. Now Mom and Robin. Pretty soon Jeremy would be the only person in the state of Ohio who'd never been on TV.

There was a knock on his door. Jeremy didn't answer.

"May I come in?" It was Dad.

Jeremy still didn't answer.

Dad opened the door. "Are you all right?"

"Yeah."

Dad came over and sat on his bed. "I know you're disappointed," he said.

Jeremy didn't say anything.

"So am I."

Jeremy looked, but he couldn't see his father's face clearly in the pale light coming from the hall.

"I was kind of hoping *we'd* be on TV tonight," Dad said.

"You were?"

"I thought a reporter would come up and ask us why we came on such a cold day. And then when I saw your Michael Jackson poster, I *knew* somebody would ask why we came."

"The poster's ruined." The light from the hall seemed to shine directly on the the bare spot where Michael Jackson used to be. Jeremy hoped his father wouldn't say "I told you so."

He didn't.

"There was a famous artist named Andy Warhol," Dad said. "And he predicted that, with television and all, everybody would be famous for fifteen minutes sometime in their life."

"Everybody?"

"For fifteen minutes," Dad reminded him.

Still, *everybody.* Even Jeremy.

"The thing is, you don't want to peak too early," Dad said. "If you have your fifteen minutes when you're a kid, what do you have to look forward to when you grow up?"

Still.

"What was that guy's name again?" Jeremy asked.

"Andy Warhol. You know, the guy who painted soup cans."

Jeremy didn't know. He must have missed Andy Warhol's fifteen minutes.

13.

Jeremy lay in his darkened room and thought.

Fifteen minutes. That wasn't much.

And the way things were going, he wasn't even going to get that. Not unless a bank robber fell in his lap or a drowning kid swam to him.

How did a slob like Chins Dankin manage to get so much publicity, year after year?

Jeremy knew the answer. Chins had a special talent. Not many people could eat nine cherry pies in ten minutes.

Jeremy wished he had a special talent.

But maybe he did.

Jeremy got up and turned on the light. He went over to his desk and got out a piece of paper. He began writing.

Things I Do Well

Then he stopped. He picked at his hangnail. He chewed on his pencil. He ripped a corner off the paper and rolled it into a little ball. He looked at the words again. What *could* he do well?

Not his homework. Not his violin.
There must be something.
Maybe he should change the title:

Things I *Like* To Do

This was easier. Jeremy started writing.

1. Go on field trips
2. Play Missile Command
3. Ride my bike (but not in the snow)
4. Play baseball (but not in the snow)
5. Hang around with Squirrel
6. Talk on the telephone
7. Chew Big Bubba
8. Collect posters of famous people
9. Suck on Cheetos (and M & M's)
10.

Jeremy stopped. This list wasn't any good, either. He knew of at least two kids in his class who'd scored higher on Missile Command. And what kind of contest could you win by going on field trips or sucking on Cheetos? Maybe, if you were rich, you could collect more posters than anybody else. But Jeremy wasn't rich.

It was no use. He turned off the light and went to bed.

Then he sat upright. He thought of it. The perfect contest. A bubble-gum blowing contest, in which he, Jeremy Bluett, would blow the biggest bubble in television history.

He could do it. He knew he could.

After breakfast the next morning he stuffed his last five pieces of Big Bubba in his mouth. He'd never chewed that much all at once before, but he needed to practice. Just getting the gum started made his jaws ache.

"What's in your mouth, Jeremy?" Mrs. Bluett asked in the car.

Jeremy didn't say anything.

Robin sniffed. "Smells like Big Bubba."

"Jeremy."

Jeremy took the gum out of his mouth and stuck it on the back of his notebook.

Mrs. Bluett looked at Jeremy through the rearview mirror. "What am I going to do with you, Jeremy?"

After Mrs. Bluett dropped them off, Jeremy popped the gum back in his mouth. It was cold and stiff and hard to chew.

"Jeremeeee," Robin said. "You're not allowed to chew gum in school."

But Jeremy didn't say anything. He couldn't, with all that stiff gum in his mouth.

It had loosened up a little by the time he saw Squirrel on the playground, but it was still too stiff to blow a bubble.

"What do you have in your mouth?" Squirrel asked.

Jeremy opened wide so Squirrel could see the wad of Big Bubba.

Squirrel whistled. "Geez Louise," he said. "How many pieces is that?"

Jeremy held up five fingers.

"Have you tried blowing a bubble with it?"

Jeremy shook his head.

"Try it."

Jeremy held up his hands to protest that the gum was still too stiff. The first bell rang.

"Hurry," Squirrel said. "Before you have to take it out."

It was now or never. Jeremy pushed his tongue through the wad, pulled it back, and blew. He thought maybe nothing would happen in this cold air, but the bubble grew in front of his nose, then his eyes. He kept blowing.

"Geez Louise!" Squirrel cried. David Jones and Kevin Johansen came over.

"Holy cow, Germy," David said. "I never saw such a big bubble."

"I've got a cousin that blows bubbles bigger than that," Kevin said. "He chews eight or ten pieces at a time."

Jeremy's bubble popped, softly, across his face.

"What a mess," David said, admiringly. "You're never going to get it off."

The boys waited while Jeremy took the rest of the gum out of his mouth and used it to dab at his face. By the time the second bell rang, his eyelashes still felt a little sticky, but everything else was okay.

As they walked into the building, Jeremy asked Kevin about his cousin. If he was going to win a contest, he'd need some competition.

"Rudy's in sixth grade," Kevin said, "and he goes to Abigail Adams." Abigail Adams Elementary School was the next school over from Dolley Madison.

"Do you think he'd be interested in a contest to see who can blow the biggest bubble?" Jeremy asked.

"Interested? He'd *win* it, no sweat." Kevin stopped. "Of course, I'd have to check with him first."

Jeremy smiled again. He could see the TV cameras already.

14.

Jeremy needed lots of practice before going up against a big blower like Rudy. That meant lots of Big Bubba.

As soon as he got home from Mrs. Carlson's house that afternoon, he emptied the coffee can where he kept his money. One dollar and twenty-seven cents.

He checked his wallet, but all he found was his library card. There was seventeen cents in the bottom of his underwear drawer.

He asked Robin how much money she had.

"Twenty-three dollars and sixty-four cents," she said.

Jeremy smiled at her.

"You're not getting a penny of it, Germy Blew It, so you can quit looking at me like that."

"I didn't say I wanted it, did I?"

"Don't get any ideas, that's all," she said. "I'm saving up for an aquarium."

Jeremy used the money in his coffee can to buy a bag of Big Bubba at Hook's Drugstore after school the next day. He knew he'd need more before the contest, but that was all he could afford right now.

Jeremy could hardly wait until he got home from Mrs.

Carlson's to pop six pieces of Big Bubba in his mouth. He watched himself, chewing, in the bathroom mirror.

He looked a little funny, almost like a chipmunk with acorns in his cheeks. But he thought he had room for more gum in his mouth. So he popped two more pieces in.

He chewed and chewed and chewed. Finally, when the wad was as soft as it was going to get, he tried pushing his tongue through a corner of it. He blew a tiny bubble while most of the gum sat in his mouth.

This was going to take a lot of practice.

He kept chewing and blowing, chewing and blowing, all weekend. By Sunday night his jaws ached, but he could handle twelve pieces at a time. And he could blow bubbles wider than his face.

"How about holding the contest on Saturday?" Jeremy asked Kevin on the playground before school Monday morning.

Kevin looked at him blankly.

"The bubble-gum blowing contest," Jeremy reminded him.

"Oh, that," Kevin said. "I don't know why you want to bother. You haven't got a chance against Rudy. I saw him over the weekend, and he can chew a whole bag of Big Bubba at a time now."

Jeremy swallowed. A whole bag. That was thirty-six pieces.

Kevin laughed. "I thought you'd give up, Germy."

"Germy doesn't give up that easily," Squirrel said. "Do you, Germy?"

Jeremy didn't say anything.

"Ha!" Kevin said. "I thought so." He laughed again and turned to join some other boys across the playground.

Squirrel looked at Jeremy, disappointed.

"Wait a minute, Kevin!" Jeremy called. "Tell Rudy the contest is at one o'clock Saturday at my house."

Kevin turned back. "You sure, Germy?"

"I'm sure," Jeremy said. "And I'm going to win."

"'Atta boy, Germy," Squirrel said.

Jeremy could see it now.

"Against all odds, underdog Jeremy Bluett beat bubble-gum blowing champion Rudy What's-his-face in a blowing match this afternoon. Jeremy blew a bubble so big that witnesses had to scramble for safety. We'll have a live interview with the new champ on our six o'clock news."

All Jeremy needed was more practice gum—and more people. Tom Boyd would never cover a bubble-gum blowing contest between just two kids.

But Jeremy didn't want any more big blowers. Rudy What's-his-face would be enough competition.

At noon Jeremy walked up to a group of third grade boys.

"Are you guys going to be in the contest Saturday?" he asked.

"What contest?" asked a boy carrying a lunch box that said BEN BRIGANTI 3-B on it.

"The bubble-gum blowing contest. To see who can blow the biggest bubble."

"A bubble-gum blowing contest?" One of the boys laughed and walked away.

But the others were interested. "What do you have to do?" Ben asked.

"Chew as much gum as you want and see who can blow the biggest bubble. Kids from other schools are going to be in it."

"When did you say it's going to be?" another kid asked.

"One o'clock Saturday. Do you want to be in it?"

Ben nodded. "Is there an entry fee?"

What a wonderful idea. If everybody paid an entry fee, Jeremy would have enough money to buy more practice gum.

"Yeah," he said, looking at Ben and trying to figure how much he'd pay. "A quarter."

Ben pulled out a wallet that showed several dollar bills. "Do you have change?"

Jeremy wished he'd made the entry fee higher. "Not right now," he said. "I'll have to get back to you."

Another kid gave him two dimes and five pennies. "The name's Scott Richmond," he said. "Mark it down."

Jeremy took out his math homework and wrote Scott's name on the back.

"Where's this contest going to be held?" Scott asked.

"At my house," Jeremy said. "1865 Bosworth Lane."

Scott wrote it down. When Jeremy saw it written down like that—*1865 Bosworth Lane*—he thought for a moment what his mother would say when she saw all those gum chewers on her carpet. Maybe he should call the whole thing off.

"I'll see you Saturday," Scott said.

Jeremy opened his mouth to say something, but nothing came out.

Squirrel came up.

"Why's everybody giving you money?" Squirrel asked.

"It's the entry fee for the contest," Jeremy said.

"You're charging an entry fee?"

Jeremy nodded. "I've got expenses."

"What kind of expenses?"

"Just expenses," Jeremy said. "This is going to be a big contest. City-wide."

"City-wide? One kid from Abigail Adams doesn't make it city-wide."

"He's not the only one. Lots of kids, from all over the place, want to be in it."

"Yeah?" Squirrel scrunched up his nose.

"Yeah." Jeremy stuck out his chin. Then he brought it back in again. "And lots of reporters'll be interested, too."

"Reporters?"

"Sure. Didn't you see the cherry pie–eating contest on TV the other night? We'll be mobbed."

Squirrel didn't look convinced.

"Which reminds me," Jeremy said. "Have you talked to Tom Boyd lately?"

"Who's Tom Boyd?"

"You know, the reporter who put you on TV."

"Oh, him. Why would I talk to him?"

"My dad says reporters like to keep in touch with their contacts."

"Contacts?"

"People they've interviewed."

"Oh." Squirrel shook his head. "I haven't heard from him."

"Maybe you should call him," Jeremy said.

"Why? What would I tell him?"

"About the bubble-gum blowing contest," Jeremy said patiently. "Tell him it's city-wide."

Squirrel's nose started to scrunch again. "You mean you're going to try to get on TV—*again*?"

Jeremy nodded. "If I don't make it this time, I'll bust."

Squirrel sighed. "All right," he said. "I'll call Tom Boyd."

15.

Jeremy stopped at Hook's Drugstore after school and bought three bags of Big Bubba.

"Three bags," Squirrel marvelled.

"This is just my practice gum," Jeremy said. "Wait until you see what I buy for Saturday."

"Why?" Robin asked. "What's happening Saturday?"

"Nothing for you to worry about," Jeremy said.

"She doesn't know?" Squirrel asked.

Jeremy shook his head. "Not exactly."

"What about your parents? You've told them, haven't you?"

Jeremy didn't say anything.

"Geez Louise," Squirrel said.

Jeremy didn't turn at Mrs. Carlson's house, the way he was supposed to.

"Jeremeeee," Robin said. "Where are you going?"

"To Squirrel's," he said. "For just a minute."

"You'll get in trouble," she warned.

"Tell Mrs. Carlson I'll be there in just a minute,"

Jeremy said. "Tell her I had to run back to school and get something."

Robin sucked in her breath and pulled herself up tall. "I cannot tell a lie," she said.

"Then don't tell her anything."

Squirrel always stayed by himself after school. He could watch anything he wanted on TV. He could eat anything he wanted out of the refrigerator. He could play anything he wanted on the Atari. He could call anyone he wanted on the phone. Squirrel didn't even know who Lawrence Welk was.

Jeremy liked to think his life would be like this next year when he and Robin stopped going to Mrs. Carlson's.

Squirrel used a key pinned inside his jacket to unlock the door. He flipped on the TV in the kitchen and opened the refrigerator door.

"We don't have time for that," Jeremy said. "We've got to hurry, before Mrs. Carlson comes looking for me."

"Okay, okay." Squirrel shut the refrigerator and went to the telephone. "Do you know the number?"

"555–2222."

Squirrel dialed just once and got it right. "Hello!" he said.

"Tell her you want to talk to Tom Boyd," Jeremy prompted.

"Oh, yeah. Could I talk to Tom Boyd please?"

Jeremy stood right next to Squirrel and could hear the taped music.

"Hey, that's neat," Squirrel said. "Just like on TV."

A voice crackled through the line, and Squirrel asked

again to talk to Tom Boyd. Jeremy crossed his fingers and hoped Tom Boyd would be there.

He was.

"Hello, this is Edward Hutchison," Squirrel said.

The voice said something, and Squirrel repeated, "Edward Hutchison. You interviewed me at Dolley Madison Elementary School a couple of weeks ago."

The voice said something else.

"Edward Hutchison," Squirrel said again. "You know, Squirrel."

The voice evidently knew.

"I just wanted to let you know about a big contest we're holding."

"City-wide," Jeremy prompted.

"It's city-wide to see who can blow the biggest bubblegum bubble."

The voice laughed and asked something.

"Who's sponsoring it?" Squirrel repeated. "Jere—"

Jeremy shook his head, violently. "Tell him . . . uh . . . we're raising money for our school."

"We're raising money for Dolley Madison Elementary School," Squirrel said.

Jeremy grinned. It sounded good.

It wasn't until Squirrel was off the phone that he realized what that meant.

"Where are we going to get money for the school?" he asked.

"From the entry fees," Squirrel said.

"But I just spent that money," Jeremy said.

"You did? Where?"

Jeremy held up the three bags of Big Bubba.

"Uh oh," Squirrel said.

They looked at the bags.

"Maybe more kids'll sign up," Squirrel said hopefully.

"I was planning to buy more gum. I'll need to practice a lot if I'm going to beat Rudy What's-his-face."

"Oh." Then Squirrel brightened. "Maybe Tom Boyd won't be able to come. He said Saturdays are usually pretty slow, but you never can tell. If something else comes up, he won't be able to come."

"But I *want* him to come," Jeremy said. "I want to be on TV, remember?"

"Uh oh," Squirrel said again.

When Jeremy got home that afternoon, there was a letter waiting for him. Robin saw it first.

"Jeremy!" she screamed. "Look!"

Jeremy looked.

It was from the White House. And it was in a small envelope, just the right size for an invitation.

"Goodness," Mrs. Bluett said. "Why would you be getting a letter from the White House?"

"Open it and find out," Robin said.

Jeremy's fingers trembled as he opened it. Maybe he wouldn't have to worry about making money for the school. Maybe he wouldn't have to go up against Rudy What's-his-face. Maybe he'd be in Washington, with the president of the United States.

"Read it aloud!" Robin demanded.

Jeremy began reading. " 'Dear Jeremy: Thank you for your thoughtful letter. . . .' "

"I didn't know you wrote the president, Jeremy," Mrs. Bluett said. "I think that's wonderful."

"Keep reading!" Robin said.

" 'America has been blessed with many riches,' " Jeremy read, " 'but none is more precious than the young people who will someday lead the world toward peace and . . .' " He stopped.

"Peace and what?" Robin asked.

" ' . . . freedom,' " Jeremy said, disgusted. He turned the paper over to make sure there wasn't anything else. Like maybe an invitation to the White House.

"What's wrong with peace and freedom?" Robin asked.

"Nothing at all," Mrs. Bluett said. "That's a lovely letter, Jeremy. You'll have to save it."

"Can I take it to school to show my teacher?" Robin asked.

"That's up to Jeremy," Mrs. Bluett said. "It's his letter."

"You can keep it," Jeremy said. He went upstairs and put ten pieces of Big Bubba in his mouth.

16.

"We're not planning to go anywhere or do anything special this weekend, are we?" Jeremy asked at dinner.

"Not that I know of," Dad said.

"Hank."

Mr. Bluett looked at his wife blankly.

"You promised to help me paint the living room, remember?"

"Oh, that."

Jeremy knew what painting day was like. "What day are you going to paint?"

"Saturday," Mrs. Bluett said.

"Uh, do you think you could do it Sunday instead?"

Mom shook her head. "We need Sunday to relax, before we start another week of work. What difference does it make to you?"

"Oh, I just wanted to have some guys over on Saturday. We're working on . . . uh . . . a school project."

Robin cocked her head and looked at Jeremy suspiciously. But Mom smiled.

"A school project?" she said. "First a letter to the

president and now a school project. I'm really proud of you, Jeremy."

"Then it's okay?"

"Of course, your friends can come here. We won't disturb you."

"Maybe we should put off painting to another weekend," Dad said.

Mom laughed. "Don't you wish."

Six more kids were waiting for Jeremy on the playground in the morning. They each gave him a quarter.

And Squirrel collected $1.25. Jeremy figured he'd stop at Hook's Drugstore after school and buy some more practice gum.

"Some of this goes to the school," Squirrel reminded him. "Don't forget."

Jeremy looked at the money in his hand. It seemed a shame to waste it—any of it—on the school. He wished he'd said they were giving it to somebody else. Orphans, maybe, or lost dogs. Anybody but the school.

Jeremy tried to think of something more pleasant. "Have you contacted the other reporters yet?" he asked Squirrel.

"What other reporters?"

"The other TV stations, the newspaper, the radio—you know, the *other* reporters."

"You want me to call everyone?"

"Somebody's got to. It would seem funny if the winner called them."

"What makes you so sure you'll win?" Squirrel asked.

Jeremy looked at him.

"Never mind," Squirrel said. "I'll call."

But what if Jeremy *didn't* win? What if Rudy What's-his-face won instead? Then Rudy would be the one on TV.

Jeremy had never met Rudy What's-his-face, but he could just imagine what he looked like. Rudy was probably a huge kid with wide, powerful jaws that worked like a trash compactor. Heck, Rudy probably *was* a trash compactor. Jeremy imagined him chewing soup cans and jars of applesauce.

But Jeremy couldn't give up now. He had to keep practicing. Chewing and blowing. Chewing and blowing. Until his jaw muscles ached and he could feel them growing.

He tried doing some of his practice chewing in school, but Mrs. Scheeler kept making him put his gum on his nose.

He tried practicing at Mrs. Carlson's house, in the bathroom. He locked the door and stuffed fourteen pieces of Big Bubba in his mouth. He stayed in the bathroom for twenty-five minutes, chewing gum and blowing bubbles. He tried to watch himself in the mirror, but the bubbles grew so big that they blocked his vision.

After a while Mrs. Carlson knocked on the bathroom door. "Are you all right, Jeremy?" she asked.

"Mmm-mmmm." With fourteen pieces of Big Bubba in his mouth, Jeremy couldn't speak.

"What? I can't understand you!"

"Mmm-mmmm-mmmmmmm."

"Please open this door immediately, Jeremy."

"Mmm-mmmm-mmmmmmm-mmmmmmm."

"That's it. I'm going to get the key."

Jeremy pulled the wad of Big Bubba out of his mouth, wrapped it in toilet tissue, and flushed it away.

What a waste.

Jeremy couldn't afford to waste any more gum, so he had to do all of his practice chewing alone in his room, with the door locked.

He could handle seventeen pieces of Big Bubba in his mouth at a time now, and his bubbles were so big that when they burst, they almost always got stuck in his hair. He had to comb his hair carefully over the sticky parts so his mother wouldn't notice.

Still, seventeen pieces were less than half a bag, and Rudy What's-his-face could chew a whole bag at a time. He wondered if Rudy What's-his-face ever got gum stuck in his hair. Probably not. His jaws were so wide—and powerful—that the bubbles didn't come close to his hair.

Besides, Rudy What's-his-face probably had a shaved head.

17.

A hall monitor walked into 5-B in the middle of reading the next morning and handed Mrs. Scheeler a note. Mrs. Scheeler glanced at it and laid it on Jeremy's desk.

Jeremy Bluett   5-B
Please report to the principal's office.

Jeremy had been to the principal's office before—the last time was to deliver the petition about cafeteria food —but he'd never been *summoned* before. This was serious.

Maybe Mrs. Scheeler had complained about all that gum. But Mrs. Scheeler was looking at him, smiling. She wouldn't do something like that.

Maybe somebody had reported that he was collecting money on the playground.

"Why don't you go and find out?" asked Mrs. Scheeler, still smiling.

Jeremy pulled himself out of his seat and headed for the door. As he passed Squirrel's desk, Squirrel patted his rear.

"Good luck," he whispered.

Usually when Jeremy got out of class to get a drink of water or go to the bathroom, he took his time and looked in other classrooms to see what was going on. But he didn't have time to look around today. He had to think.

He tried to figure how much money he'd collected so far—$2.25 on Monday and $1.50 on Tuesday. Plus the $1.25 Squirrel had collected.

So far, he'd spent $4.71 on gum. But some of that was his own money.

Maybe if he promised to pay everybody back . . .

The school secretary nodded when he showed her the note. "You may go in now," she said. "Ms. Morrison is expecting you."

Jeremy just bet she was.

Ms. Morrison smiled when Jeremy walked into her office. "Hello, Jeremy," she said.

Jeremy concentrated on a piece of fuzz on the carpet.

"I hope I didn't frighten you with my note. Some students get nervous when they're called to the principal's office." She laughed a little.

So did Jeremy. But he kept his eyes on that piece of fuzz.

"I just wanted you to know how pleased I am with the way you're channeling your energies now," she said. "This is much more constructive than circulating petitions."

He looked at her.

"You didn't think I knew, did you?" She smiled. "I'll admit I had to do quite a bit of digging to find out who was behind this contest. They didn't say on the radio who had organized it. "

"It was on the radio?"

Ms. Morrison nodded. "One of those community service announcements."

On the radio!

"When I heard it, I was just overwhelmed. To think that someone would want to help his school so much. And to think he didn't even want any recognition for it."

"He didn't?"

"Maybe we'll be able to arrange a field trip after all. And maybe we'll be able to purchase some new audiovisual equipment and—"

"Uh . . . how much does a field trip cost?"

"It depends on where you go. Some places are free, but we still have to pay for the bus. And that's usually around a hundred dollars."

A hundred dollars. Jeremy gulped. "Uh . . . we might not make that much money."

Ms. Morrison smiled. "Oh, I know. But I'm just so *overwhelmed*. To think that you'd do this for your school. To think that you cared so much."

To think that she wanted a hundred dollars.

Robin threw up Thursday night.

"She probably has what Jeremy and Mrs. Carlson had," Mrs. Bluett said. "She'd better not go to school tomorrow."

Jeremy offered to stay home and take care of her.

"That's very generous of you," his mother said. "But there's no emergency at the office tomorrow. I can take the day off."

Jeremy was glad Robin wasn't at school the next day when Ms. Morrison included news about the contest in her morning announcements over the public address system. That afternoon Jeremy collected $5.25 in entry fees.

David Jones and Michael Taylor signed up, but Kevin didn't.

"It's no use," Kevin said. "Nobody can beat Rudy."

"Phooey," David Jones said. "I don't believe your cousin chews a whole bag of Big Bubba at a time. *Nobody* could do that."

"Well, maybe it's not a *full* bag," Kevin said, "but it's a lot!"

Jeremy looked at him. It wasn't a *full* bag? He felt his own jaws moving, as strong and sure as a trash compactor.

Jeremy bought four bags of Big Bubba on his way to Mrs. Carlson's house. That left seventy cents for the school. He'd worry about Ms. Morrison and the field trip later. First he had a contest to win.

When he got home, he locked the door and popped eighteen pieces of Big Bubba in his mouth.

He chewed and chewed and chewed. It took a lot of chewing to get eighteen pieces of Big Bubba soft enough to blow a bubble.

Finally he blew. His first bubble popped across his face, and some of it got stuck in his hair. He'd have to remember to comb his hair back tomorrow.

He chewed some more, without bubbles, just to loosen up. It was important to stay loose. He didn't want to go into the contest tomorrow with a stiff jaw.

He blew another bubble. This one was beautiful. It was big and sturdy, the kind of bubble that could beat Rudy What's-his-face, hands down.

Jeremy kept chewing and blowing, chewing and blowing. By the time his mother called him for dinner, he was glad to take the gum out of his mouth. His jaws were aching, and he was getting sick of the sugary sweetness of Big Bubba.

Mrs. Bluett dished out spaghetti for dinner. Spaghetti was normally Jeremy's favorite meal. But tonight the spaghetti tasted like Big Bubba, soft and squishy and sweet. Even his milk tasted like Big Bubba.

"What's wrong, Jeremy?" his mother asked. "You've barely touched your spaghetti."

Jeremy wrapped some spaghetti around his fork and tried to show some enthusiasm for it.

"Are your friends still coming tomorrow to work on the project?" Mom asked.

Jeremy stuffed the spaghetti in his mouth and nodded.

"Well, I'm sure we'll be able to stay out of each other's way." Mrs. Bluett turned to her husband. "Did you remember to pick up the paint?"

His father nodded. "I'm all ready for a weekend of fun and excitement."

Jeremy swallowed his spaghetti. "Aren't you afraid the smell will make Robin sicker?" he asked.

"That's a good point," his father said. "Maybe we should put this off for a week or so."

"Not a chance," Mrs. Bluett said. "Robin's feeling a lot better tonight. She hasn't thrown up all day."

Robin burped just then, and Jeremy looked at her hopefully. But she didn't throw up.

18.

By the time Jeremy woke up in the morning, his father had already shoved the furniture to the center of the living room and was spreading plastic drop cloths on the floor.

His mother had removed pictures from the living room walls and was filling the nail holes with Spackle.

"Good morning, sleepyhead," Mrs. Bluett said. "I hope none of your friends' parents come to the door." She was wearing paint-splotched jeans and one of Dad's old shirts. A red bandana held back her hair.

Mr. Bluett, with unshaved whiskers on his chin, was wearing old plaid pants and an Ohio State sweatshirt with holes in the elbows.

Painting day was even worse than Jeremy remembered. "Uh, Mom," he said, "are you *sure* you couldn't could do this another day?"

"Are you kidding?" she said, waving her arm around the room. "After we've gotten this far?"

"Even I want to get it over with now," Dad said.

"Don't worry," Mom said. "We won't say a word to

77

your friends, and you can just pretend that we're the hired help."

"I hope we're getting paid a lot," Dad said.

Jeremy hovered in the hallway near the living room while his parents painted. His father pushed the paint roller across the wall with wide sweeping motions, and his mother fussed over the baseboard trim. Dad finished the first wall, and Jeremy checked the clock. Ten forty-five. They seemed to be making good time. Maybe they'd finish before the contest.

Then he noticed that his mother wasn't painting anymore. She was standing in the middle of the room, with her chin in her hand, looking at the wall Mr. Bluett had just finished.

"Hank," she said, "come here a minute."

"Oh, no," Dad said. "You do this every time."

"Just come here a minute," she said.

He came.

"It isn't right," Mom said. "I think it's too yellowish."

"No," Dad said. "It's Almond Cream."

She shook her head.

"It's close enough to Almond Cream," he said.

"It's yellow."

"I've always liked yellow," Dad said. "It reminds me of sunshine."

Mom shook her head.

Dad sighed. "Do we have to change clothes, or can we just go like this?"

"It's a paint store," Mom said. "We'll put on coats and hope we don't meet anyone we know."

Jeremy looked at the clock. It was eleven fifteen. In one hour and forty-five minutes the TV cameras would be here.

"You can't go!" Jeremy cried. "You've got to finish before the contest!"

"What contest?" Dad asked.

"He means the *project*," Mom explained. "Don't you, Jeremy?"

"Uh . . . right."

"Don't worry," Mom said. "Just take the boys up to your room."

"There might be some *girls,* too," Jeremy warned. He didn't think so, but there might.

Mom laughed. "Is that what's got you so upset? Then clean up your room. And, don't worry, we'll be back before anyone gets here."

Jeremy put fifteen pieces of Big Bubba in his mouth and gave his room the best cleaning it ever had. He even scraped the smushed 3 Musketeers bar off his desktop.

The candy bar had been there since Halloween, and it looked pretty sickening. The Big Bubba didn't taste so great, either. Maybe it was because the smell of paint had followed him up the stairs to his room.

Jeremy took the gum out of his mouth without blowing a bubble.

It was almost twelve o'clock. He didn't feel like eating, but he decided to fix peanut butter and jelly sandwiches so he and Robin could get lunch out of the way before the contestants arrived.

He'd finished the sandwiches and was setting out the paper plates when the doorbell rang.

"Jeremeeee!" Robin came running from her room. "Somebody's at the door!"

"I know," Jeremy said. "Be quiet and maybe they'll go away."

Robin slapped her hand over her mouth.

Jeremy looked at the clock. It was 12:06. Too early for any of the contestants.

The doorbell rang again. And again.

"What'll we do?" Robin whispered.

"I'll go see who it is," Jeremy said.

"Don't open the door!" Robin cried. "It might be a kidnapper!"

Then she slapped her hand over her mouth again.

"Don't worry," Jeremy said. "I'm not going to open the door." He ran upstairs and looked down from the bathroom window to see who it was.

It was Ms. Morrison. In the flesh.

19.

Jeremy watched Ms. Morrison press the doorbell one more time before she started pounding on the door.

"Hal-loo?" she shouted. "Is anybody home?"

Jeremy ran down the stairs and opened the door.

"Oh, Jeremy," Ms. Morrison said. "I was beginning to think that nobody was home."

"My parents went to the store," he said.

"And we're not supposed to answer the door when they're not here," Robin said righteously.

"That's a very good rule," Ms. Morrison agreed. "But do you think it would be all right if *I* came in?"

Jeremy looked at Robin. "I guess so." He stepped back and let the principal come in.

He could tell she was surprised when she looked around the living room.

"My parents are painting today," Jeremy said uneasily.

"So I see."

"My mother thought the Almond Cream looked too yellowish," Robin said. "So they took it back to the paint store."

Jeremy didn't know what to do. Maybe he should offer Ms. Morrison a seat. But the chairs and sofa were covered with plastic drop cloths.

"Would you like to come in to the kitchen?" he asked.

Ms. Morrison nodded, still surprised—almost dazed, Jeremy thought.

"We're having sandwiches," Jeremy said. "Do you want one?" He opened a cabinet and looked for one of the tin cans that his mother sometimes made fancy sandwiches from.

Ms. Morrison seemed to come out of her daze. "That sounds good. Let me help."

Before Jeremy could find a can, Ms. Morrison took out a couple of slices of bread and began spreading peanut butter on both of them. As if she made peanut butter and jelly sandwiches all the time.

"That's not the way my mother does it," Robin said. "She puts peanut butter on just one piece of bread. And then she puts jelly on the other."

Jeremy shot Robin the meanest look he could muster.

Ms. Morrison just smiled. "My mother used to make them that way, too," she said. "But I find that putting peanut butter on *both* slices—and jelly in the middle—keeps the bread from getting soggy."

Jeremy tried not to stare. He tried to act as if school principals made peanut butter and jelly sandwiches in his kitchen all the time.

Ms. Morrison took a bite out of her sandwich, just like a regular person. "The contest *is* today, isn't it, Jeremy?"

Jeremy nodded and looked at the clock. "In about forty-five minutes."

"What contest?" Robin asked.

"Does anyone want some potato chips?" Jeremy asked quickly.

"No, thank you," Ms. Morrison said. "I thought I'd come a little early to help set things up." She glanced toward the living room. "I see there's a lot to be done."

Robin took a handful of potato chips from the bag. "What contest?" she asked again.

Ms. Morrison looked at Robin, then at Jeremy. "She doesn't know?"

"She's been sick," Jeremy said.

"I'm sorry to hear that."

"Will somebody please tell me—what contest?"

"Why, it's a bubble-gum blowing contest," Ms. Morrison said, tearing a paper towel off the roll by the sink to dab at her mouth. "Jeremy here came up with the idea as a way to raise money for the school."

Robin's mouth fell open. "Jeremy's raising money for the school?"

"Yes, we want to pay for a field trip and a filmstrip projector and—"

"I don't think we'll make that much money," Jeremy reminded her.

"I'm sorry," she said, smiling. "I can't help but dream."

Jeremy nodded.

"But, Jeremy, where were you planning to hold this contest?" Ms. Morrison asked.

"Yeah, Jeremy," Robin said. "Where?"

"My mom said I could have it up in my room," Jeremy said.

Ms. Morrison looked doubtful. "How big is your room?"

"Big enough." He hoped.

Jeremy's parents came home just as they were finishing lunch.

"Sorry we're a little late," Mom said. "There was an accident on . . ." She stopped when she saw Ms. Morrison.

"Hello," Ms. Morrison said, extending her hand. "I'm Judith Morrison, the principal at Dolley Madison."

"Oh . . ." Mrs. Bluett touched her hand to the bandana holding back her hair.

Dad took Ms. Morrison's hand. "I'm Hank Bluett and this is my wife, Sally. I think we met at Parents' Night."

"I'm sorry for bursting in on you like this," Ms. Morrison said. "I wanted to be here for the contest today."

"The contest?" Dad said. "Oh, you mean the project."

Mrs. Bluett's hand fell from her bandana to her open mouth.

"Jeremy's having a bubble-gum blowing contest here to raise money for the school." Robin grinned, waiting to see her parents' reaction.

"A bubble-gum blowing contest?" Dad repeated.

"Here?" Mom's hand went back to her bandana.

"When?" they both asked.

Jeremy looked at the clock. "In about twenty-five minutes," he said, softly.

"This is your school project?" Mom checked.

Jeremy nodded.

"You should be very proud of Jeremy," Ms. Morrison said. "He's shown a lot of initiative in this project."

"He certainly has," Mr. Bluett said.

"Jeremy," Mom said, in an even voice, "how many children are you expecting?"

"I don't know."

"I would guess between fifty and a hundred children

from our school," Ms. Morrison said. "I don't know about other schools."

"Between *fifty and a hundred*?" Mom repeated. That surprised Jeremy, too. He could never fit that many in his room.

"Other schools?" Dad repeated.

Jeremy could explain that. "It was announced on the radio. I guess you didn't hear it."

"On the radio?" Mom gasped.

"Squirrel called a couple of radio stations."

"I suppose some of these kids will be bringing their parents?" Mom asked.

"That would be my guess," Ms. Morrison said.

Mom's other hand went up to her bandana.

"I'm terribly sorry about this inconvenience," Ms. Morrison said. "I thought about having the contest at the school, but I didn't want to take it away from Jeremy. It was such a *lovely* gesture on his part."

"Just lovely," Dad said.

The doorbell rang. Robin ran to the window.

"Michael Taylor is here!" she cried. "And his mother!"

Mrs. Bluett looked around the living room, draped with plastic drop cloths. "Oh no!" she said.

20.

Fifty-nine boys and seven girls entered the contest, but three of the girls left when they saw all those boys.

Ms. Morrison stood with Jeremy at the front door and collected quarters from the ones who hadn't paid yet.

"Is he on the list?" she would ask Jeremy, as if there were a list of people who'd paid. Jeremy remembered the boys in his own class, and he remembered Scott Richmond, whose name he'd written on his math homework. But he had trouble remembering the others. It was especially hard with the third graders. They all looked alike. And, of course, he didn't know who had paid Squirrel. If a kid said he'd paid, Jeremy didn't argue with him.

Most of the kids brought parents with them, and a few brought little brothers and sisters. The kids all complained about the smell of paint, but the grown-ups just looked surprised.

Three boys started playing King of the Mountain on a stepladder, but the game ended when Mr. Bluett put the ladder away.

One toddler found an open can of spackling and started to eat it.

Mrs. Bluett took the mother to the kitchen to call the Poison Control Center.

"Why don't we create a nursery somewhere for the little ones?" Ms. Morrison suggested.

"They can go up to Robin's room," Jeremy said.

"Mom . . ." Robin started toward the kitchen.

"I mean, *my* room," Jeremy said. "But you have to stay with them," he told Robin. "And don't let them touch a thing."

"I won't." Robin smiled, very sweetly. "I can't wait till this is over. You're really going to get it."

Jeremy kept watching for Rudy What's-his-face, and he almost missed him. Rudy didn't look at all like a trash compactor. He was skinny and wore glasses. And his last name was Miller.

"How many pieces of gum can you chew at a time?" Jeremy asked.

"I don't know," Rudy said. "Maybe six or seven."

"But Kevin said you chewed a whole bag at a time."

"Kevin lies a lot."

This contest was going to be a cinch. All Jeremy needed now was Tom Boyd with his camera and microphone.

When Squirrel sauntered in at 12:59, Jeremy pounced on him.

"Where are they? Where are they?" he asked.

"Who?" Squirrel said.

"The reporters!"

"What?" Squirrel said. "I can't hear you!"

"The reporters!" Jeremy shouted over the noise of the crowd. "Where are they?"

"You mean they're not here? Are you sure?" Squirrel looked around. "How can you tell in this crowd?"

"Don't you think I'd notice if somebody had a big TV camera?"

"TV cameras aren't that big," Squirrel said. "Maybe that guy with a videocamera is a TV reporter."

"No," Jeremy said. "He's just a father. He came with three kids. Where are the reporters? You said there'd be lots of them."

"Wait a minute," Squirrel said. "*I* never said there'd be lots of reporters. You're the one who said that. I just called them, like you told me to."

"Well, where are they?"

"How do I know? Maybe they got busy. Maybe there's a big fire somewhere or something."

"Or maybe you just *said* you called them."

"You were there when I called Channel 2."

"How do I know you really called Channel 2? Maybe you just called the lady who gives the time."

"That's not fair," Squirrel said. "I never wanted this crummy job in the first place. I just—"

"Excuse me, boys!" Ms. Morrison shouted over the noise of the crowd. "It's after one o'clock! I think we'd better get started!"

"Can't we wait just a minute?" Jeremy shouted back. "Maybe somebody can't find the house."

"What? I can't hear you!"

Jeremy started to yell louder, but Ms. Morrison took him by the hand and moved through the crowd toward the stairs. "Is there a bathroom here?" she shouted.

First peanut butter and jelly sandwiches, and now this. Jeremy was certainly learning a lot about school principals today. He pointed toward the little powder room under the stairs.

Still holding on to Jeremy's hand, Ms. Morrison

worked her way toward it. To his surprise, she pulled him into the bathroom with her.

There he was, with a toilet, a sink, and the school principal.

"Now we can talk," Ms. Morrison said. "What were you trying to say?"

Jeremy couldn't remember. He couldn't think of anything but the toilet, the sink, and the school principal.

"Then let's get started," Ms. Morrison said.

Jeremy suddenly remembered what he was going to say. "Maybe we should wait a little, in case somebody's having trouble finding the house." Somebody like Tom Boyd, he thought.

There was a knock on the bathroom door.

"Just a minute," Ms. Morrison called. Then she turned back to Jeremy. "We don't have *room* for anybody else," she said. "This house is full, upstairs and down."

There was another knock on the door. Jeremy knew she was right. "Okay," he said. "I'll go get my gum."

"You're entering the contest?" Ms. Morrison looked surprised.

"Sure."

"The person who organizes a contest usually doesn't enter it," she said.

She had to be kidding. "Why not?"

"For one thing, the other contestants wouldn't consider it fair," she said. "And, besides, you'll be too busy."

"Doing what?" Jeremy asked.

"Judging," she said. "And handing out prizes."

Prizes. Jeremy's stomach took a nosedive.

"You do have prizes, don't you?" Ms. Morrison asked.

Jeremy just looked at her.

"Let's not worry about that now," she said. "I'll think

of something. And I've got a metric ruler in my bag."

"What for?"

"To measure the bubbles." She smiled. "I thought you'd forget that. But I never imagined you'd forget the prizes." She shook her head. "Not everyone is as unselfish as you, Jeremy. Not everyone wants to help the school. Some children just came to win a prize."

Jeremy could tell she was getting overwhelmed again. Fortunately, there was another knock on the door.

"Come on," Ms. Morrison said. "We have to get this show on the road."

She started to open the bathroom door. Jeremy held back.

"Now what?" she asked.

Jeremy didn't say anything. It was hard to explain how he felt about having other kids see him come out of the bathroom with the school principal.

21.

The crowd became quiet when Jeremy emerged from the bathroom with Ms. Morrison. At first Jeremy's stomach lurched with the thought that everyone was watching them, but then he saw they were all looking toward the front door. And he heard a familiar voice.

". . . from Channel 2 News," the voice said. "Believe it or not, we're here to cover the bubble-gum blowing contest."

Mr. Bluett moved through the crowd, with his hand extended. "Hi," he said. "I'm Henry Bluett. Let me show you where you can set up your equipment."

The crowd parted for Mr. Bluett as he led Tom Boyd and his cameraman into the living room. Then mothers closed in on their children to wipe lunch off their faces and run combs through their hair.

"We're going to be on television!" somebody said. "I don't believe it!"

The rest was like a dream. Working under bright lights, the cameraman followed Jeremy as he moved from the kitchen to the living room, up the staircase and into the bedrooms, measuring bubbles. He shot the pictures from over Jeremy's shoulder, so Jeremy knew his face wouldn't be on TV. But his hands would.

Jeremy liked the way the crowd parted when he approached a contestant with his metric ruler. And he liked the way Ms. Morrison wrote it down when he called out the measurement.

The only thing he didn't like was the way his mother looked when he saw her. She was holding the kid who'd swallowed the spackling, and she was trying to tuck wisps of hair under her bandana.

A girl—Jennifer Lounsberry from the sixth grade—won. Her bubble measured 22 centimeters at its widest point. She did it with nineteen pieces of Big Bubba in her mouth.

Still, Jeremy thought he could have beaten her.

Ms. Morrison said the prize was that Jennifer would get to read the announcements over the school's public-address system every morning for a week.

Just thinking about reading the announcements to the school—*the whole school*—made Jeremy sure he could have won.

But he wondered what the prize would have been if Rudy—or somebody else from another school—had won. Maybe Ms. Morrison would have talked the other principal into letting the winner read the announcements at that school, too.

Tom Boyd had Jennifer blow another bubble for the camera. Then he asked Ms. Morrison about the contest.

"It was the brainchild of one of our fifth graders, Jeremy Bluett," she said. "We raised just four dollars and fifty cents today, but Jeremy had already raised another eleven or twelve dollars through entry fees paid earlier in the week. That may not sound like much, but . . ."

It sounded like a lot to Jeremy. Ms. Morrison expected him to give the school eleven or twelve dollars. Where was he going to get that much money? After everything that had happened today, he didn't think his parents would loan him a used piece of dental floss, let alone eleven or twelve dollars. He thought of all the Big Bubba he'd bought and chewed in the last week. And his stomach began to hurt again.

Then the moment came. Tom Boyd turned to Jeremy, and so did the camera.

"Why did you want to raise money for your school, Jeremy?" Tom Boyd asked.

Jeremy looked at the camera.

He looked at the lights.

He looked at the microphone.

Then he threw up.

22.

"Don't worry about it," Mrs. Bluett said as she led Jeremy to his room. "These things happen. You've probably just got what Robin and Mrs. Carlson had." She stopped. "But I thought you'd already had that."

Then she told Robin to take the little kids to her own room.

"But, Mom . . ." Robin began.

"No buts about it. Jeremy just threw up on television."

Robin herded the little kids out, quickly.

Mrs. Bluett found Jeremy some clean clothes. Then she started to leave, too.

"Mom," Jeremy said.

She turned.

"I'm sorry," he said. "I never should have done this without asking. Especially on painting day."

Mrs. Bluett pursed her lips, as if she might have an M & M in her mouth. But Jeremy knew she didn't. He knew this was a real pursing, and he expected a real lecture.

But she didn't lecture. She stopped pursing her lips

and smiled, faintly. "Considering everything that's happened," she said, "I'm glad we had the drop cloths down."

Jeremy heard parents come up the stairs to fetch their children from Robin's nursery.

"Thank you for taking such wonderful care of Wanda," one mother said. "I hope your brother feels better soon."

Several other parents told Robin they hoped her brother felt better, too.

But Jeremy had no intention of feeling better—ever again. Once, when they were in second grade, Squirrel had thrown up in front of the class. But nobody—*nobody* —ever threw up on television and went out in public again.

"I will never leave this room again, as long as I live," Jeremy said aloud.

"I don't blame you," said a familiar voice from the hall. "You really did a number on my microphone."

The voice waited, but Jeremy didn't say anything. He tried not to breathe, even.

"May I come in?" Tom Boyd asked.

Jeremy still didn't say anything.

"Okay," Tom Boyd said. Jeremy could hear his footsteps walking away.

"No, wait!" Jeremy cried.

The footsteps stopped.

"You can come in," Jeremy said.

The footsteps came back, and the door opened a crack.

"Are you sure?" Tom Boyd asked.

Jeremy nodded.

Tom Boyd came in and looked around. "Somehow I knew you'd have posters of famous people in your room." He pointed to the blank spot on the wall. "What happened there?"

"Michael Jackson used to be there," Jeremy said, but he didn't tell what had happened to him.

And Tom Boyd didn't ask. "I just wanted you to know that we won't use that last part of the tape," he said.

"Thanks."

"And," Tom Boyd said, "I wanted to congratulate you on finally getting me out here. I didn't even know you were behind it until I got here. That's the mark of a great PR man."

"PR man?"

"You know, a public relations man, like a publicity agent. All the big stars have them." He nodded toward the posters on Jeremy's wall. "They'd all be nobodies if they didn't have somebody like you, planning things and getting publicity for them."

"Stars need publicity?"

"Are you kidding? Do you think it's easy to get your face on TV?"

Jeremy shook his head, violently.

"You'll be a great publicity agent someday, kid." Tom Boyd winked. "You just need to develop a better stomach for it."

Jeremy heard the last contestants leave, and the house became quiet. Unnaturally quiet. He was glad his stomach still hurt. It gave him an excuse to stay in his room, away from his parents. He figured the less they saw of him, the better.

Then he heard his father's steps on the stairs.

Jeremy pulled the covers over his head.

But his father kept coming. Sure enough, he stopped at Jeremy's door.

"May I come in?" he asked.

"Yeah," Jeremy said. He might as well get it over with.

Mr. Bluett came in and sat down on the bed. "I was proud of you today, Jeremy," he said.

"Proud?" Jeremy pulled the covers off his head and looked at his father. *"Proud?"*

Dad nodded. "Right after I got over being mad."

Jeremy could understand the mad part, but not the proud.

"You did something I've always wanted to do," Dad said.

"Hold a bubble-gum blowing contest?"

Dad shook his head. "Step into the spotlight."

"Huh?"

"I know this sounds silly," Dad said, "but I've always thought of myself as a famous person that nobody knows about. I think that's why I wanted to be a reporter. I wanted to interview important people, rub elbows with them. And I wanted to see my name in print—*by Henry Bluett.*" He sighed. "But then I found out about all the boring stuff reporters do. All the meetings they have to cover. And what they get paid."

"Peanuts," Jeremy said, and his father nodded.

"So now I work in advertising, and I help the newspaper make its money so reporters can get their bylines." Mr. Bluett spoke in a soft, wistful voice that Jeremy had never heard before.

"At least you don't get paid peanuts," Jeremy reminded him.

"No, I get walnuts, and that's not a whole lot better."
Dad stood up. "But I've got a son who knows what he
wants and goes out to get it."

"But Tom Boyd said they aren't going to use the end
of the tape," Jeremy said.

"No, but someday somebody else will use another tape
with you in it. Remember Andy Warhol. You've still got
your fifteen minutes coming."

Jeremy grinned. "So do you, Dad."

Jeremy went downstairs to watch the Channel 2 news
at six o'clock. The contest story didn't come on until the
very end, after the weather and sports.

Finally, though, he saw himself on the screen, measuring bubbles with Ms. Morrison's metric ruler. Jeremy was
surprised to see that more than his hands showed up on
the screen. He could see the entire back of his head—
which was interesting, because he had never seen it before. Once the camera even showed the side of his face.

The camera paused on the side shot while Tom Boyd
read,

"The bubbles were carefully measured by Jeremy Bluett,
a fifth grader at Dolley Madison who planned and carried off
the entire event without any adult help."

"Does he have to remind me?" Mom asked.

"Jeremy held the contest after the school had to cancel
planned field trips because of budget cuts. Dolley Madison's
principal, Judith Morrison, said she didn't think they'd raised
enough money today for a field trip, but she appreciated
Jeremy's effort.

"Unfortunately, Jeremy became ill before the afternoon's festivities were over, and we weren't able to interview him."

Tom Boyd looked at the camera and smiled.

"But WQQP-TV has a surprise that may make Jeremy feel better. We've decided to arrange a tour of our studios for Jeremy's class. The station will pay for all expenses connected with the trip—proving once again that Channel 2's for you."

"Did you hear that?" Robin said. "Jeremy got a field trip for his class!"

Jeremy grinned. Maybe his whole face hadn't been on TV—maybe it never would be—but he'd gotten Tom Boyd to cover the contest and he'd gotten a field trip for his class.

He was turning into a great PR man.

23.

The telephone kept ringing all evening. Squirrel called. David Jones called. Even Mrs. Carlson called.

"I always knew you were a wonderful boy," she said.

Then Ms. Morrison called.

Jeremy's stomach trembled when he heard her voice. She probably wanted the school's money.

"How are you, Jeremy?" she asked.

"I'm okay," he said, holding his stomach.

"Isn't Channel 2's generosity wonderful?" she said. "I'm just so overwhelmed!"

"Me, too," Jeremy said.

"This means your class will be able to go on a field trip —and we'll be able to use the contest money for something else!"

Jeremy was afraid he might throw up again.

"I know we didn't make much, but . . ."

He had to tell her.

"I don't have the money."

"That's all right, Jeremy. We don't have to decide right away what we're going to do with it. I just thought it would be nice to mention in Jennifer's announcements Monday morning. Several people have already . . ."

"I don't have it. I've only got seventy cents. I spent the rest."

There was a pause. "You *spent* it?"

"But I'll figure out how much it was, and I'll pay you back. Honest."

"What did you spend it on?"

"Big Bubba."

"Bubble gum?"

"For the contest."

"Well, if it was a legitimate contest expense . . ."

"No," Jeremy said, "it was for me. I wanted to win the contest so I bought a lot of practice gum."

"I see."

There was silence on the other end of the phone. Jeremy waited.

"This is pretty serious, Jeremy," Ms. Morrison finally said. "The contestants thought their money was going for a good cause."

"I'll pay it back. I'll think of something."

"I'm sure you will, Jeremy," Ms. Morrison said. "I'm sure you will. I've never met such a resourceful young man."

Jeremy's picture was in *The Advocate-Journal* the next morning. It was another side shot, of him measuring Jennifer Lounsberry's bubble.

"I didn't know somebody from the newspaper was here," he said.

"That's what's nice about newspaper people," Mr. Bluett said. "They're unobtrusive."

101

Jeremy didn't know what *unobtrusive* meant, but it made his mother laugh, and that was enough for him.

His parents finished painting the living room that afternoon. The Almond Cream came out right this time—which was a good thing, because the paint store was closed.

Mrs. Bluett wore one of Dad's old shirts and her paint-splotched jeans again. But not the bandana. She put on makeup and used the curling iron before they started.

"You never know who's going to stop by," she said.

Jeremy spent the afternoon crawling around the house looking for stray wads of gum. Whenever he found one on the carpet, he rubbed it with ice, the way his mother told him to. Then he scratched at the cold wad with his thumbnail until the gum flaked off and could be thrown in the wastebasket.

Normally Jeremy would have hated a job like that—especially the day after being sick. But he liked doing it today—almost as if he were earning his way back into the family. If he could only think of a way to earn eleven or twelve dollars for the school.

Mrs. Bluett said she was too exhausted to even think about fixing a regular meal Sunday night. So Mr. Bluett went to Rocco's Pizza Parlor and brought home a mushroom and pepperoni pizza. They sat down and ate it on the drop cloths in the living room.

"Do you think maybe I could have an advance on my allowance?" Jeremy asked.

"Oh, no," Mrs. Bluett said. "Not another project. I don't think I can take it."

"No, it's not another project," Jeremy said. "I just have a few contest expenses to take care of."

"He owes the school eleven dollars and twenty-five cents," Robin said.

"Where'd you get a figure like that?" Jeremy asked.

"It's simple," she said. "There were sixty-three kids in the contest yesterday, right?"

Jeremy nodded.

"I multiplied sixty-three by twenty-five cents. Then I subtracted the money you took in at the door." She smiled triumphantly. "That leaves eleven dollars and twenty-five cents."

"I don't get it," Dad said. "How did the contest end up costing you eleven bucks?"

"It's hard to explain," Jeremy said.

"No, it's not," Robin said. "Jeremy used the entry fees to buy Big Bubba for himself."

"You bought eleven dollars worth of Big Bubba?" Dad asked.

"You *chewed* eleven dollars worth of Big Bubba?" Mom asked.

"I didn't chew *all* of it," Jeremy said. "And I didn't spend all of the entry fees, either." He looked at Robin. "I still have seventy cents left."

"Okay," she conceded. "But you still owe . . ."

"Ten dollars and fifty-five cents," Dad said.

"Think of all that Big Bubba." Mom held her jaw. "His poor teeth."

"I was practicing—you know, keeping my jaws limber —for the contest." Jeremy looked at his parents. "I guess you won't give me an advance."

"Bingo," Dad said.

"But what'll I do?"

"You'll have to think of a way to earn the money on your own," Dad said. "Maybe you could shovel the neighbors' sidewalks."

Jeremy had tried that before. It was cold work.

"Or you might think of something else," Dad said.

"That's what I'm afraid of," Mom said.

But Dad was right. He *might* think of something else. Something he could do really well.

Upstairs in his room that night, Jeremy took out a sheet of paper and wrote at the top

Things I Do Well
(and people would be willing to pay for)

This time he didn't have to pick at his hangnail or chew on his pencil. There were lots of things he could do.

1. Bring television cameras and newspaper reporters to the event of your choice
2. Organize contests
3. Arrange field trips
4. Contact world leaders
5. Make peanut butter and jelly sandwiches that won't get soggy
6.

Jeremy stopped writing and looked at his list. He knew he'd have no trouble earning $10.55.

But why stop at $10.55?

If kids paid a quarter apiece to enter a city-wide bubble-gum blowing contest, how much would they pay to enter a state contest? Or a national? Heck, he could hold the International Bubble-Gum Championship Blow-Off.

This was only the beginning.

"PR tycoon Jeremy Bluett stopped by our studios this evening to share his secrets of success. He says he began his journey to fame and fortune deeply in debt. We'll have a live interview with Mr. Bluett at eleven."